Wishbone took a ste[p]
and then froze. He had he[ard]

Whipping his head around, Wishbone strained his ears. The sound was distant, but—

"Help!"

It was Sam's voice. She sounded as if she was in trouble!

Wishbone barked.

Joe stopped and looked back. "What's up, Wishbone? Find another frog?"

With a low bark, Wishbone looked around at Joe, then back the way they had come.

"Help!"

There it was again!

Wishbone barked more and started to run back.

Joe followed the terrier. "What's the matter?"

By that time, Wishbone was running full tilt. "It's Sam! She's yelling for help! Come on, Joe!"

Books in The Adventures of WISHBONE™ series:

Be a Wolf!
Salty Dog
The Prince and the Pooch
Robinhound Crusoe
Hunchdog of Notre Dame
Digging Up the Past
The Mutt in the Iron Muzzle
Muttketeer!
A Tale of Two Sitters
Moby Dog
The Pawloined Paper
Dog Overboard!
Homer Sweet Homer
Dr. Jekyll and Mr. Dog
A Pup in King Arthur's Court
The Last of the Breed
Digging to the Center of the Earth
Gullifur's Travels
Terrier of the Lost Mines
*Ivanhound**

Books in The Super Adventures of WISHBONE™ series:

Wishbone's Dog Days of the West
The Legend of Sleepy Hollow
Unleashed in Space
Tails of Terror
*Twenty Thousand Wags Under the Sea**

*coming soon

The Adventures of WISHBONE™

TERRIER OF THE LOST MINES

by Brad Strickland and Thomas E. Fuller

Inspired by *King Solomon's Mines*
by H. Rider Haggard
WISHBONE™ created by Rick Duffield

Big Red Chair Books™, *A Division of Lyrick Publishing*™

This book is a work of fiction. The characters, incidents, and dialogues are products of the authors' imagination and are not to be construed as real. Any resemblance to actual events or persons, living or dead, is entirely coincidental.

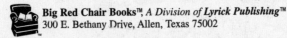 **Big Red Chair Books**™, *A Division of* **Lyrick Publishing**™
300 E. Bethany Drive, Allen, Texas 75002

©1999 Big Feats Entertainment, L.P.

Edited by Kevin Ryan

Copy edited by Jonathon Brodman

Continuity editing by Grace Gantt

Cover concept and design by Lyle Miller

Interior illustrations by Don Punchatz

Wishbone photograph by Carol Kaelson

Library of Congress Catalog Card Number: 98-88463

ISBN: 1-57064-278-8

First printing: November 1999

10 9 8 7 6 5 4 3 2 1

For my big sister, Juanita Merck
—Brad Strickland

This book is dedicated to my sister,
Dianne Allen, and her husband, Chip.
Marriage can be an adventure, too.
—Thomas E. Fuller

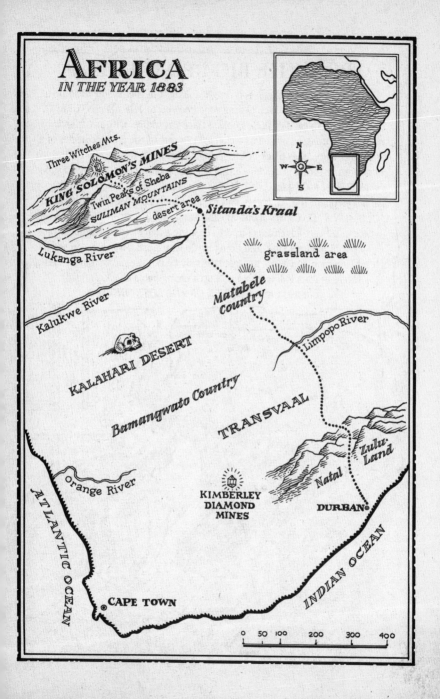

FROM THE BIG RED CHAIR . . .

Oh . . . hi! Wishbone here. You caught me right in the middle of some of my favorite things—books. Let me welcome you to THE ADVENTURES OF WISHBONE. In each of these books, I have adventures with my friends in Oakdale and imagine myself as a character in one of the greatest stories of all time. This story takes place in the spring, when Joe is twelve and he and his friends are in the sixth grade—during the first season of my television show.

In *TERRIER OF THE LOST MINES*, I imagine I'm Allan Quatermain, an old elephant hunter, trader, and explorer from H. Rider Haggard's *KING SOLOMON'S MINES*. It's about an expedition into unknown parts of Africa, where four brave adventurers travel—crossing a fierce desert, confronting a one-eyed murderous king, and doing battle with hostile warriors—in search of a missing man and a lost treasure that may be nothing more than a legend.

You're in for a real treat, so pull up a chair, grab a snack, and sink your teeth into *TERRIER OF THE LOST MINES!*

Chapter One

Wishbone pushed his doggie door open, stuck his head outside, and took a deep sniff of a beautiful Saturday morning. "Ah—dew on the grass! Spring leaves on the trees! No pesky cats! Perfect!"

The white-with-brown-and-black-spots Jack Russell terrier took a step into his backyard and stretched.

"It's almost the best time of the day! The sun is just up, the air is fresh, and I'm ready for anything. Especially breakfast."

Wishbone scratched his ear thoughtfully. For some reason, Ellen and Joe Talbot, the people he lived with, didn't share his joy of waking up with the dawn on weekends. Oh, well, he could have some play time by himself while he waited for them to get up and prepare his breakfast. As he thought of play time, Wishbone remembered his brand-new squeaky toy.

"I left it out here somewhere." He sniffed his way across the yard and suddenly stopped. He felt cold all over. The scent he was picking up told him a story. "A strange dog! Right in our yard! How could I have slept through that?" Two more sniffs. "And, uh-oh, he's got my rubber bone. *My* bone! I've got to get to the bottom of this!"

Following the scent, Wishbone trotted around to the front yard, then next door, past Wanda Gilmore's house, and down Forest Lane. The strange dog had come this way—and so had Wishbone's rubber bone! The scent cut across yards and headed toward the center of Oakdale. It grew stronger all the time, too. Wishbone knew he was hot on the trail of the thief.

The trail led him behind Rosie's Rendezvous Books & Gifts, into a narrow alley. Wishbone concentrated hard, moving along with his nose to the ground. A snarling growl made him skid to a stop.

There was the thief, right ahead—and he was twice Wishbone's size! He was a shaggy brown mongrel, without a collar. *Uh-oh,* Wishbone thought. *A stray dog, and a tough one, too!* The brown dog barked a warning.

Wishbone approached cautiously. "Easy, easy, big guy. Hey, new in town? Just visiting, or—" As soon as he was close enough, Wishbone snatched his bone from the

ground. Then he turned around so fast that he almost did a somersault, and he dashed up the alley. Behind him he could hear the mongrel's angry bark, then the clatter of nails on the pavement. The chase was on!

Wishbone had been thinking, and he had a plan. But, for the plan to work, he had to be a little faster than the other dog—and the other dog had longer legs! As Wishbone turned the corner in front of Rosie's, he knew very well that the brown dog was getting closer.

Wishbone saw that some construction work was being done. Just down Oak Street, workers had dug a hole. A yellow-metal fence surrounded it, and big wooden boards covered it. The fence could keep people out, but a dog of the right size just might squeeze through! Wishbone made his way in just inches ahead of the bigger dog. He heard the other animal's surprised, angry growl as it charged after him and got stuck in the fence.

Wishbone ran across the boards and dove through the fence on the other side. He knew the other dog wouldn't be stuck in the fence for long. Already he heard the stray barking at him from half a block away. Still, he had put some distance between himself and the mongrel. Would it be enough? . . .

It wouldn't. The stray dog managed to get loose and ran even faster. Wishbone thought hard. What other trick could he use? Then Wishbone spotted a small sports car, a red convertible, parked at a curb up ahead. Perfect! He could dive under the car. The larger dog would never be able to get his paws on him!

The terrier flattened himself into a running crouch. Then he sped under the driver's side of the parked car. He waited to hear the angry grunt as the stray got stuck. Instead, he heard the slap of paws on concrete and a furious bark. Suddenly, he found himself almost nose to nose with an angry and very large dog!

Whoa! How'd he get on the passenger's side so quickly? He must have jumped right over *the car!* Wishbone hastily turned around and headed for the driver's side, but then changed his mind. Just as the stray leaped over the car again, Wishbone came out under the front of the car. He ran down Oak Street as fast as his legs could go!

He was away from the center of town, heading down a residential street. He was running so hard, his lungs felt as if they were on fire! Wishbone knew he had to take a moment to rest. But he had to find a safe place.

The Wilsons' house was on the corner. A tall, wooden fence surrounded their yard. Wishbone made a hard right, his paws scrabbling for traction. He ran to the fence and pushed a certain board with his nose. It bent to the right, just in time for him to dive through!

He held his breath as he heard the other dog rush by. Then he dropped his rubber bone and took a few deep breaths. "Can't take long, though. He's a dog, just as I am! His nose will soon tell him he's on the wrong track!"

Wishbone grabbed his bone again. He knew the other dog would come back any second. Wishbone had to find a place where he could lose the bigger animal.

Pushing the board aside with his nose, Wishbone hopped back onto the sidewalk. He looked down the block. At that moment, he saw the stray dog turn and come running back! Wishbone began to run. "I can't keep up this pace all the way home and stay ahead of him. Jackson Park—that's my only chance for safety!"

Wishbone cut across a couple of yards. Then he made another hard right turn. All the time, the stray dog was gaining, but slowly. The other dog had not taken a rest, but Wishbone had. Jackson Park, a grassy, open area, had playground equipment, winding trails, trees, and bushes. It had a lot of good places to hide. Maybe it would also have a lot of people because it was Saturday. And most people in Oakdale knew Wishbone and would help him.

Except Wishbone had gotten up very early.

To his disappointment, Wishbone saw that Jackson Park was deserted. The other dog was now only a couple of yards behind him. He was no longer barking, but saving all his energy for the chase!

The swings were ahead. Wishbone hurled himself into a flying leap. His front paws hit the seat of a swing, and it arced up into the air while he held on tight. The big dog ran right under him before the swing swung back and Wishbone jumped off. He ran back the same way he had come.

Again, Wishbone had gained a little ground, but he was getting tired. The bigger dog had anger driving him now. With a furious scrabble of paws, he reversed direction and barked. What trick could Wishbone pull to—

"Big! Stop that!"

A woman jogger was heading right for Wishbone. He heard the other dog suddenly stop running. He turned to see the animal drop his head.

"Sit!" commanded the jogger, who wore a blue sweatsuit. A water bottle on a long strap was slung around her left shoulder. "Sit, Big!"

The dog named Big sat.

Then Wishbone recognized the jogger. She was . . . "Officer Garcia! Good morning! Great to see you! Now— do your duty!"

The athletic, dark-haired woman was Officer Rosa Garcia of Oakdale Animal Control. She came up to Big, shaking her head. "You bad boy! You climbed over your fence again, didn't you? Come along with me. I'll call your owner."

Officer Garcia took the strap from her water bottle and used it as a leash. Big gave Wishbone one mean look. Then, his tail wagging in defeat, he walked off with Officer Garcia.

She looked back at the terrier and said, "You'd better get home, Wishbone, before you get into trouble."

Wishbone wagged his tail. "Great idea!"

He trotted back home, feeling proud.

"What an adventure! An all-out race against long odds, and once more Wishbone comes through! I wonder if breakfast is ready."

Wishbone heard voices as he got near the Talbot house. Joe's best friends, David Barnes and Samantha Kepler, were there. Wishbone picked up his pace. He went inside through his doggie door and dropped his rubber bone in a safe corner. Then he found Joe and his friends at the breakfast table.

"Hi, buddy," Joe said, getting up from a chair and reaching into a cabinet. "Ready to eat?"

Wishbone hurried to his dish. "Always! Pour away, Joe!" Wishbone licked his chops as Joe filled his dish with kibble. Then he dove in.

"So," David said, "this is a yearly event. And no one's found it yet."

"Not yet," Sam agreed. "Miss Gilmore offered a prize of a hundred dollars in savings bonds ten years ago for any kid in the sixth-grade class who could find it, but no one's got the prize yet."

"Well," Joe said, sitting back down at the table, "*we* haven't tried yet. Okay, David, what do we know?"

David shrugged. "Not a whole lot. More than a hundred and fifty years ago, when Oakdale was just a small village, a large group of people got together and started a new town. It was about ten or twelve miles southeast of here. It was called Willow Bend, and it was built at the edge of the Willow River."

"That wasn't such a great place to live, as it turned out," Sam added. "About five years after Willow Bend was established, a terrible flood wiped out the town one spring. Most of the houses were washed away. Even the town's businesses were ruined. A few people were injured, but no one was killed. Then most of the thousand people who had lived in Willow Bend moved here, to Oakdale. The town was never rebuilt."

Wishbone was all ears. He finished the last crumb of his kibble, licked his chops, and went over to sit at Sam's feet. She reached down and scratched his ears—a perfect way to end a meal, in Wishbone's opinion!

"So what exactly has everyone been looking for?" Joe asked, finishing a glass of milk.

"A cornerstone," David said. "The town hall of Willow Bend was just about to be built when the flood hit. The commemorative cornerstone had been made and put in place. It served as part of the foundation, and it was inscribed with the town's name. Then Willow Bend was washed away. As Sam said, even the town's stores and shops were damaged so badly that they either collapsed or had to be torn down. The cornerstone was still supposed to be in the same place, though. It was on a hill, and the flood didn't move it."

Sam nodded. "In the 1890s, people still knew where it was. But somehow since then everyone just forgot about the cornerstone and the town itself. Through the years all traces of the town have disappeared. People lost track of where the town had really been built. The Oakdale Historical Society would like to find the location of the cornerstone. That would give society members a good idea of exactly where Willow Bend was, and how the town was laid out. But, unfortunately, no one has been able to locate it."

"And that's why Miss Gilmore began to offer the prize to the sixth-graders ten years ago," David added. "She's held the contest every year since then, but no one has ever found the cornerstone."

Wishbone squirmed with pleasure as Sam scratched exactly the right spot behind his left ear. "A mystery. A mystery of history. I'm up for it!"

"Okay," Joe said, standing and picking up his friends' breakfast dishes. "I think the best way to start this hunt is by talking to Miss Gilmore. Help me clear the table, and we'll get going."

Sam and David helped Joe put the dirty dishes into the dishwasher, while Wishbone supervised. He cocked his head thoughtfully. "You know, this reminds me of something. A history mystery. Something that once was very well known but became lost. And it took a group of brave adventurers to face all the dangers and find it. Now, what was that . . . ?"

He didn't have time to wonder about it at the moment. Joe, David, and Sam went out the back door. Wishbone rushed to follow them. The sun was high and warm. In the yard next door, Wanda Gilmore was watering her flowers.

Wanda wore a big sun hat, and she hummed as she watered her prized petunias. She looked up with a smile as Joe, Sam, David, and Wishbone came over. "Good morning!" she said with a wave. "I'll just bet I know why you're up so early on a Saturday. This time every year sixth-graders get the same look on their faces. You're getting ready to earn that prize, aren't you?"

Joe laughed. "We're going to give it a try, Miss Gilmore. We thought we'd start by asking you for any clues you might have."

Wanda sighed. "I don't have very many. I can tell you where to look, in a general way. The Willow River has changed its course over the years, and we're no longer sure exactly where the big bend used to be. Five years ago, though, some students found traces of what might be old building foundations. The place is about ten miles southeast of here. Let me get a map, and I'll show you." She put down her watering can and gave Wishbone a hard stare. "No digging while I'm gone!"

Wishbone looked up innocently. "Digging? Me?"

Wanda went inside for a few moments. Then she returned, unfolding a map. "Here we are," she said, bending down and spreading the map open on the ground. Joe, David, and Sam bent over to look at it.

"I see the Willow River," David said. He put his finger down on the right-hand corner of the map.

"The best way to get to the general area is by taking this road," Wanda said, pointing. "All this area is farmland now. The farmers know about the contest, so they won't mind if you look around on their property. Just don't go into any pastures where there are bulls. The foundations—if that's what they really are—were found right in this area, where this stream runs into the river."

"Could we borrow your map?" Sam asked.

Wanda shook her head. "I'm sorry, Sam, but this is really the official map. It's where I make notes about the places students search each year. But I have copies that I hand out and you're welcome to use. I'll go get one."

While Wanda went back inside, Joe studied the lower right corner of the map. Spaces had been shaded off in light green, yellow, pink, and orange. "I guess all these places have been well searched," he said. "And I see that Miss Gilmore's put a red X here, where someone found something."

"That's probably where we should start," David said.

Sam shook her head. "I don't know. If the foundations were discovered five years ago, you know people have looked there for the town hall cornerstone."

"Well, at least it's a place to begin," Joe said.

Wanda came out again with a copy of the map. She handed it to Sam. "You might want to mark the places on this one," she said, giving Sam a pencil.

Wishbone sat and watched Sam carefully copy the markings from Wanda's map. He was deep in thought. *A missing historical place. A copy of a map. Three brave adventurers getting ready to go on a search. I* know *this reminds me of something.*

He scratched his chin. *It's so familiar. . . . Oh, of course! This is just like the great adventure novel* King Solomon's Mines, *by H. Rider Haggard!*

As Wishbone sat in the warm sun, he began to remember H. Rider Haggard's tale of high adventure. Solomon, the son of David, was king of Israel from about 960 B.C. to 925 B.C. According to legend, his great wealth came from secret mines in Africa. Nearly three thousand years later, in 1883, an English explorer and hunter named Allan Quatermain found himself on a quest for those mines. Wishbone began to imagine that he was Allan Quatermain, who tells the tale of the great search for the lost mines of King Solomon. . . .

Chapter Two

Sir Henry Rider Haggard was just the man to write an adventure story like *King Solomon's Mines*. Haggard was born in England, but he spent a good part of his life in Africa. He loved stories of adventure. In 1884, his brother made him a bet. He bet that H. Rider Haggard could not write an adventure story that would be as popular as Robert Louis Stevenson's great novel, *Treasure Island*. Haggard won the bet with *King Solomon's Mines*, an exciting adventure tale told by the main character, Allan Quatermain. . . .

It is odd that an old elephant hunter, trader, and explorer like me should suddenly become an author and take pen in paw to write a book. I have good reasons, though. First, my friends Sir Henry Curtis and Captain John Good asked me to. Second, an old wound that I received years ago when a lion mauled my leg flared up again after my last adventure. I will be in the hospital in Africa for some time while it heals. Writing will give me something to do! Third, my son is off in London, studying to be a doctor, and I want him to know the whole story.

Fourth and last, this is the strangest story I know. And it all happened to me, Allan Quatermain, of Durban, the capital city of Natal province on the southeastern coast of Africa.

It all began eighteen months ago, in late November, 1882. I had been hunting big game up near Bamangwato country, five hundred miles north-northeast of Cape Town. The Bamangwato area is a dry land almost in the center of southern Africa, and there I had bad luck. Everything went wrong. At the end of the hunting season, I had shot no game, had come down with a case of fever, and was running low on money. So I hitched my oxen to my wagon. With my tail between my legs, I drove them to Cape Town, a large city near the very southern tip of Africa. There I sold all the gear I didn't need, including my wagon and oxen. Then, feeling quite sad, I bought a ticket to sail for Durban on the *Dunkeld*. It was a steamship that sailed along the African coast. The ship wouldn't leave for two days, I was told. However, to save money, I stayed aboard, instead of checking into a hotel.

On the day we were to sail, two Englishmen who had just arrived in Africa came aboard. One was Sir Henry Curtis. He was a tall, strongly built man with shoulder-length blond hair and a beard. He reminded me of a Viking. Something about him seemed to say "I was born to have adventures!" Sir Henry wore a khaki safari jacket and trousers, boots, and a white pith helmet.

His friend was named John Good. The moment I saw him, I knew he was a navy man. He was short, rather heavyset, and clean-shaven. He wore a hunting suit of brown tweed, with a hat to match, and boots. He also had a monocle—a single eyeglass—in his right eye. His teeth gleamed white and even. I learned later they were false teeth. All in all, he was the most well groomed, most direct man I had ever met.

As we sailed from Cape Town, I stood on deck, my front paws on the polished rail. November is late spring in the Southern Hemisphere, and I could smell the sweet odor of mimosa growing in the gardens of Cape Town. The navy man, whom I hadn't yet met, came over to stand beside me. "John Good," he said, introducing himself.

"Allan Quatermain," I told him.

He squinted at me through his monocle. "Ah . . . I know that name. The brave hunter."

"No," I said. "The *cautious* hunter. Brave hunters die very young, you see."

Good laughed. He held out his hand, and I put my paw out to shake. With a nod, Good said, "I'm so pleased to meet you. I myself am a captain in the English Royal Navy, retired. You see, when I turned thirty-one, I was promoted from commander to captain. My commanding admiral told me flatly that was the end of the line for me. No more promotions, he said, because I was too honest. When my superior officers asked for my opinion, I gave it to them. Shortly after my promotion, I decided to retire."

"I see," I told him. "And now you are in Africa on pleasure or business?"

"I am in Africa," he said, "because my friend Sir Henry asked me to come with him. And speaking of him, I know he would be very glad to meet you. Could you come see us in his cabin tonight, after dinner? It's a most important matter. There may be a job in it for you."

"I'm not leading any more hunting safaris for now," I told him. "My luck on the last one was all bad."

"It isn't a safari we had in mind," Captain Good said with a wink. "Something much more mysterious."

21

Well, that was quite a bone to dangle in front of someone with my curiosity! I decided that it just might be worth my while to speak to Sir Henry. I told Captain Good that I would certainly meet them after dinner.

At eight that evening, as the *Dunkeld* made its steady way eastward along the coast of Africa, I shook hands with the tall, bearded Sir Henry Curtis. He was sitting in a chair, drinking mineral water, and he asked what I would like.

"Water will be fine," I said. Without saying a word, Captain Good poured some water into a cup and put it in front of me.

"So," Sir Henry said, taking a sip from his glass, "your name is Allan Quatermain. You must be the same man who was trading around Bamangwato somewhat more than two years ago."

I perked up my ears. "Why, yes, I was. I'm surprised you know that."

Captain Good looked at me through his monocle and said, "While you were there, you met a man named Neville, didn't you?"

"Yes," I told him. "We traveled together for a week. I got a letter from a lawyer about Neville last year, asking what I knew of the man. I answered it to the best of my ability."

Sir Henry stood up and took a folded piece of paper from his breast pocket. "You wrote to my lawyer, Mr. Quatermain, and he sent your letter to me. You said Mr. Neville left Bamangwato on May 1. He was in an ox-drawn wagon, and his guide was a Zulu tribesman named Jim. You said they were going northeast, heading for the

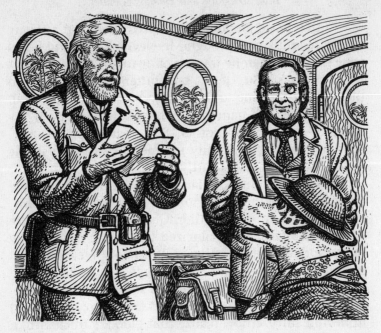

last trading post in Matabele country. From there, he planned to head on foot northward into unknown territory." Sir Henry put the letter back into his pocket. "Mr. Quatermain, do you know why Neville was heading into the unknown?"

I scratched my chin with my hind paw. This was tricky ground. A man's business is his own. So, not knowing why Sir Henry was asking, I decided to answer carefully. "I may have heard something," I said.

Captain Good nodded. "You may as well tell Mr. Quatermain the whole story," he advised Sir Henry. "I can tell he knows how to keep a secret."

Sir Henry nodded and sighed. He sat down, his eyes on the floor. "Very well," he said. "I certainly want your advice, Mr. Quatermain, and your help, if you can offer it. Mr. Neville was, in fact, my brother."

"Ah," I said. Suddenly I realized there was a strong family resemblance, though Mr. Neville's hair and beard were brown. "Then he was traveling under a false name."

"He was," Sir Henry said bitterly. "He wished to make it hard for me to find him, you see. And it was all my fault. His real name is George Curtis, and he is my younger—and only—brother. Five years ago, we quarreled. It was a foolish family argument. I was partly in the wrong, but George was partly in the wrong, too.

"Soon after that, our father died. He had never made out a will. So all the family fortune came to me. Foolishly, I refused to offer my brother, George, any share of the inheritance until he apologized to me. He was equally proud and refused to apologize. With only a few hundred pounds of his own money, George left England and headed here to Africa. He came to seek his own fortune, or so he said. That was three years ago. I have not heard from him since. I now realize that blood is thicker than water. I'd offer half my fortune if I could find George alive and well."

"But you were never willing to offer it before, Henry," Captain Good snapped, his eye gleaming behind his monocle. "Not until it was very late in the game. Now, Mr. Quatermain, perhaps you can tell us why the man you knew as Mr. Neville headed into unknown parts of Africa."

I took a drink or two of water. "I heard that he was searching for the lost diamond mines of King Solomon," I said slowly.

"King Solomon's mines!" said Sir Henry, stroking his blond beard. "Where are they?"

"No one knows," I told him. "Years ago, I think I glimpsed the mountains that border them. But there were a hundred and thirty miles of desert between me and them. I have heard that only one European ever made it across that desert. Now, I will keep your secrets, if you will keep mine. May I have your word that you will never tell anyone what I am about to reveal to you?"

"Absolutely," Sir Henry said.

"Yes, of course," said Captain Good.

"Very well," I said. "When I was a very young hunter, I heard from older men about the Suliman Mountains. They are an undiscovered range to the north. That sounds very much as if it could be 'Solomon's Mountains,' don't you think? Anyway, not long after I had come to Africa, I was near the desert I spoke of. At that time, a Zulu friend of mine told me an Englishman was dying in a village nearby. I hurried there and found that the man was really Portuguese. He was an explorer named José Silvestre. He *was* dying, but he told me he had traveled across the desert and back."

"Looking for the mines?" asked Captain Good.

"And following a map," I said. "He told me that about three hundred years ago, his ancestor had made his way to the mines. That ancestor died, but not before he had made a map. That map had been passed down to Silvestre. Before he died, he gave it to me."

"Do you still have it?" Sir Henry asked me.

"I don't have the original with me, but I do have a copy." I checked the pockets of the brown hunting jacket I was wearing. No map. I even removed my tan pith helmet and looked inside. Still no map. Then I remembered. It was in a pouch attached to a leather cord around my neck. I pulled the pouch out, opened it with my teeth, and removed a rolled-up sheet of paper. "The original was drawn in 1590 by a dying Jorge del Silvestra, the ancestor of José. He drew it by using his own blood, on a sheet of linen torn from his shirt."

"This is a very strange story, indeed," Captain Good said, as he peered through his monocle at the map.

I rose to go. "If you do not believe me, give me back the map," I said. "I am not the kind who tells lies just for enjoyment."

Sir Henry put his huge hand on my shoulder. "Please be seated, Mr. Quatermain," he said. "We do not doubt your word. You must admit, though, that the story certainly is odd."

"It is," I said, sitting again. "However, let me tell you the rest of it. When I met your brother, George, his guide was a local man who had adopted the English name of Jim. I kew Jim very well. He was a good, honest man and a fine guide. Jim was one of the Zulu people. They are the bravest and strongest warriors in southern Africa. On the morning when the two of them were getting ready to leave, Jim told me they were searching for the lost mines of King Solomon. I told him I was afraid the mines were just part of a foolish story.

"'No story, Mr. Quatermain,' Jim told me. 'I once knew a woman who came from there and got to Natal with her child. She is dead now, but she told me the mines are real.'"

"Ah," Sir Henry said. "And what did you tell Jim?"

I shook my head. "I did not have time to tell him much, but I did sketch out the map on a piece of parchment paper. 'Here,' I said to Jim. 'Give this to Mr. Neville the day you reach the edge of the desert. It may help you find a small oasis halfway across. It should have a good supply of water. You'll need it by the time you cross the desert. Good luck to you both.'"

"And then?" asked Captain Good.

"And then I never heard from Jim or from Mr. Neville again," I said. "That is all I know."

Sir Henry said, "Mr. Quatermain, I am going to look for George. I intend to trace him to Suliman's Mountains. If necessary, I will climb those mountains and go on until I find him—or until I know he is dead. Will you come with me?"

As I had told Captain Good, I am naturally cautious. In all the years I had lived in Africa, I had never once been tempted to follow the map myself. To do so seemed like certain death. Even more, what if I followed the map successfully, only to find that the lost mines were imaginary—nothing but a legend? The map led through rugged country, where large prides of lions roamed. It led across a dry, rock-strewn desert where there was no water, and perhaps deadly snakes. And it led into completely unexplored territory where anything dangerous might be hiding. The risk was great, and the reward uncertain.

"No, thank you, Sir Henry," I said at last. "I am too old to go on wild-goose chases. What if we all end up like my poor friend Silvestre? I cannot afford to die just now, you see. I have a son in England who is in medical school. He depends on my support."

Captain Good and Sir Henry both looked disappointed. Then Captain Good nudged his friend. "Half your fortune, you said, Curtis?"

Sir Henry smiled grimly. "You're right, Captain Good. Mr. Quatermain, I have far more money than I can spend. I am going to see this quest through. If you will agree to guide us, you may name any fee you wish. I will pay you before we even start out on our journey. In fact, I will arrange matters so that if anything should happen to you, your son will receive a guaranteed income until he finishes his schooling. You may organize every detail of our safari, and I will pay all the expenses."

"What if we find King Solomon's mines?" asked Captain Good, with a wink at me.

Sir Henry shrugged. "If we do, Mr. Quatermain, then you and Captain Good may share all the diamonds we find. I am rich already and do not want them. In short, Mr. Quatermain, you may name your own terms."

I could see he was being completely honest with me. I said, "Sir Henry, this is the most generous offer I have ever received. No hunter or trader would sneeze at it. But this is the hardest job I have ever been offered. I have to have some time to think it over. I will give you my answer when we reach Durban."

"Very good," said Sir Henry.

I left him and went to my cramped cabin. I lay down and fell asleep. That night I dreamed about fields of diamonds—and about poor José Silvestre, who had been a long time dead.

It took five days to sail up the southeastern coast of Africa from the Cape of Good Hope to Durban. The shoreline of Africa ran straight eastward for two hundred miles. Then it turned northeast for almost another four hundred. All the time we were traveling to Durban, I was thinking of Sir Henry Curtis's offer. Though I did not speak of the quest for King Solomon's mines to Sir Henry or Captain Good, I told them many hunting stories—all true. Many hunters exaggerate their experiences, but I did not, for so many strange things happened, anyway.

The coast of Natal was lovely. There were red-sand hills and wide sweeps of vivid green. The shore was dotted here and there with the circular villages that the Africans called kraals. They were made up of pens for the cattle and huts for the people. A ribbon of white surf bordered the shores. It spouted up in bursts of foam when it hit the rocky coast. I leaned on my paws, licked the salty spray from my muzzle, and watched the beauty of coastal Africa slide past.

And I thought about Sir Henry's offer.

At last we sailed into Durban, and it was time to make my decision. I trotted to the cabin where Sir Henry and Captain Good waited.

"Well, Mr. Quatermain, have you decided?" Sir Henry asked. "Will you give us the pleasure of your company on a journey to King Solomon's mines?"

I circled on a nearby rag rug before settling down in front of the two men. I would have given anything for a good English beef bone to chew on, but the time for action had come. There was no putting off the decision. I said, "Yes, gentlemen, I will go."

"Splendid, sir!" Captain Good said, smiling his approval of my decision. His monocle made his right eye seem unnaturally large, but it looked cheerful. "And what are your terms?"

"They are simple. Sir Henry, you will pay all expenses for the trip. You will also pay me five hundred pounds for my services. In return, I will serve you faithfully until you choose to give up the expedition, or until we succeed or fail."

Sir Henry nodded, stroking his blond beard. "Is that all, Mr. Quatermain?"

"One last thing. I'd like you to write out a legal agreement. If I die, you'll pay my son, Harry, who is studying medicine in London, the sum of two hundred pounds a year for five years. By that time he ought to be able to earn a living for himself. That's all, I think, and I'm sure you'll say it's quite enough, too."

"No," answered Sir Henry. "I accept your terms gladly. I would have paid more than that for your help."

I sat up on my rug, offered him my paw, and we shook on the deal. But as I looked into his open, noble face, I couldn't help saying, "I must tell you, Sir Henry, I make this decision because I like you and Captain Good. I think we will work well together. But if we attempt to make our way into the Suliman Mountains, I doubt we can come out of the expedition alive."

"Then why do you want to go?" Sir Henry asked in a puzzled voice.

I held my muzzle high. "Two reasons, sir. First, if fate says I am to die in the Suliman Mountains, well, then I will die in the Suliman Mountains. Second, I am poor. I have hunted in Africa all my life, and I have very little to show for it. This way my debts will be paid, and my son will be taken care of. That's it in a nutshell."

"And it's to your credit," Sir Henry said with a warm smile. "I admire you, Mr. Quatermain, for taking the job even when you feel like that about it. Either way, I'm going through with the journey to the end, sweet or bitter. If we are going to die, all that I have to say is that I hope we shall have some time first for a bit of challenging big-game hunting—eh, Good?"

"Oh, yes," said the captain. "All three of us have faced danger and have held our lives in our hands in many ways, so it is no good to turn back now."

So it was settled. For good or for bad, for life or for death, we were going in search of King Solomon's mines.

Chapter Three

The next days were busy as we put the expedition together. Until we set out, we stayed at a local hotel. Most of the job fell to me. I worked like a dog with two tails, trying to chase both at once. Using Sir Henry's money, I bought most of our supplies. The first was a wagon—a real beauty. It was twenty-two feet long, with iron axles, very strong, very light, and built entirely of well-seasoned stinkwood. It was half-tented, canvas-covered only over the last twelve feet. That was where we would sleep. The open-ended front was for the food, ammunition, and equipment we would carry.

Next, I bought a team of twenty Zulu oxen. They were small and light and perfect for living off the land. The short, heavyset Captain Good proved to be very useful. He must have been a good navy man. He could do a little bit of everything. He had some medical knowledge and could also cook, so he helped out by buying our medicines and food. Meanwhile, I stocked up on our weapons—heavy elephant guns, repeating rifles, and Colt revolvers. As a hunter, I knew our lives might depend on top-quality firearms.

Finally, I tried to hire a guide who would drive the wagon and help around the camp. I could find no one qualified, or willing to go. Then, on the evening before we were to set out, I was told there was a man who wanted to speak to me.

I jumped up into a chair in my room and perked my ears up so I would look properly alert. Soon a very tall, handsome Zulu man came in. As tall and muscular as Sir Henry Curtis, he towered over me. He puzzled me, for he was not wearing the typical Zulu tribal clothing of leopard skin. Instead, he wore a khaki shirt, khaki trousers, and boots, though he carried a traditional African walking stick. Somehow he did not quite seem to be an average Zulu. The man lifted his stick in greeting and waited. I did not rush into conversation. Zulus believe people who talk too much or too soon have no dignity. For about three minutes we simply looked at each other. When the man finally smiled and nodded, I knew it was time to speak.

"Well," I said at last, "what is your name?"

"Macumazahn, my name is Umbopa," answered the man in a slow, deep voice.

"Macumazahn is my African name," I said, impressed. "It means 'the man who keeps his eyes open.' How did you know my name?"

Umbopa stared straight into my eyes. "Everyone talks about you, Mr. Quatermain."

Well, I thought, *I could take* that *several different ways!* "I hope they speak well of me," I said. "Now, what do you want, Umbopa?" I asked, casually scratching my ear with my left hind leg.

"It is this, Macumazahn. I hear you're going on a great expedition far into the north with the white men from over the water. It is a word?"

By that, he meant "Is this true?" I nodded seriously. "Yes, it is."

"I also hear that you'll go even to the Lukanga River, far beyond the Matabele country. Is this also a word, Macumazahn?"

Whoa! I thought. *That was supposed to be a complete secret.* Sitting up straighter, I said, "And why do you ask?"

Umbopa said, "It is this, Macumazahn. If indeed you travel so far, I would go with you."

He was an impressive man. Something, though, bothered me, like the tickle of a flea crawling in my ear. How had he learned where we were going?

Stalling for time, I asked, "Where are you from? What is your kraal?"

That would tell me much, for to a Zulu his kraal is more than his village. It is also his family, his way of life—almost his personality.

Still looking me straight in the eye, Umbopa said, "I am with the Zulu people, yet I am not one of them. My people were left behind when the Zulus came south a thousand years ago. I have no kraal. I came here to learn the white man's ways. Now I am tired and am ready to go north again. Here is not my place. I want no money, but I am a brave man. I will be worth the supplies and food I use." He paused for a moment, then said, "Now I have spoken."

I was puzzled by this man. He did not want to be paid, and he seemed much too self-confident to be any ordinary ox driver. Then, too, he knew far too much about our business.

Still, I knew that having no driver meant having no expedition. I fetched Sir Henry and Captain Good and told them what Umbopa had said. Sir Henry stood next to him to look him in the eye. I noticed they were equally tall, both well over six feet. Next to them, Captain Good looked almost small. Both Sir Henry and Umbopa had a kind of noble look, too, like two proud lions.

As if reading my mind, Captain Good said, "They make a good pair, don't they? One's as big as the other."

"I like your looks, Mr. Umbopa," Sir Henry said. "You may be our driver."

"It is good," Umbopa replied with a glance at Sir Henry's own great height and strength. "We, too, are men, you and I."

I won't write everything about our long and weary trip up to Sitanda's Kraal, where the Lukanga and Kalukwe rivers met. To me, most of the area was unknown territory, in the center of the southern bulge of the African continent. It was far north of the Bamangwato country, my old unlucky hunting grounds.

We left Durban in January, at the height of the fierce African summer. The route we took over mountains and across grasslands was more than a thousand miles long. For the first seven hundred of those miles, we rode in our ox cart. Then we reached the rolling grassy hills, with their twisted, flat-topped thorn bushes. We saw baobob trees, which had leaves only three months out of the year. For the rest of the time, their bare, branching twigs made the baobobs look as if they grew upside down, with their roots spread in the air.

Our trail wound across high purple-gray ridges of stone where tse-tse flies buzzed in our ears. The bite of this fly was deadly to oxen, and we decided not to risk losing our animals. So in the second week in May we sold our oxen in the last trading post in the Matabele country.

Finally, in June, after a tiring journey on foot of another three hundred miles, we made camp. It was at the eastern edge of a vast, shallow bowl of sand and stone, a desert that shimmered with heat. Barely visible in the far distant west were two rounded volcanic domes, much taller than the other mountains around them. They were the twin peaks of Sheba, in the Suliman Mountains. The peaks wore crowns of gleaming white snow.

"There, Sir Henry," I said, pointing dramatically with my nose. "Those are the Suliman Mountains. Beyond them are King Solomon's mines."

"My brother should be there. If he is, I shall reach him somehow," said Sir Henry in a tone of quiet confidence. He raised his head, the sunlight gleaming on his blond hair and blond beard.

"Is it truly to that land you travel, Incubu?" asked Umbopa, using the blond and bearded Sir Henry's native name, which meant "lion."

Sir Henry nodded. "Yes, Umbopa."

Umbopa squatted and gazed across the rolling sands. A few lonely patches of grass grew here and there. I could see the ragged gray-green shapes of a number of scattered welwitschias, which looked much like piles of dead, dried-up leaves. However, the plants were alive, and they grew very slowly in the dry sands.

After a few moments of silence, Umbopa took a handful of dust and pebbles and let them fall to the ground. "Our path will be hard. The desert is wide. There is no water. The mountains are high and covered with snow. No one knows what is beyond them in the place where the sun sets. How shall you travel, Incubu, and why do you go?"

Sir Henry stood next to Umbopa and pointed to the

distant mountains. "I go because I believe my brother has gone there. I go to find him."

"It is a far journey, Incubu," Umbopa said, standing and striking his broad chest. "I will go with you across the desert and over the mountains. I will not trick you. I make no plots. But I know things that I must not say now. If ever we cross those mountains, I will tell what I know. For now, I will say this: Death waits there. Be wise and turn back. I have spoken." Without another word, he lifted his walking stick and returned toward the camp.

"That is an odd man," said Sir Henry, as he watched Umbopa walk away.

"Yes," I answered. "Too odd. He knows something he isn't telling us. Still, I suppose it is of no use to argue with him. We are in for a curious trip. A mysterious Zulu—adopted Zulu, rather, since he says he is not really one of them—won't make a great deal of difference one way or another."

I took a long sniff and smelled the dry air of the desert. Maybe it was my imagination, but I thought I could even smell the frosty scent of snow on those distant mountains.

"We'll make it all right," I said.

Well, I would prove to be half right.

We started out across the trackless desert. Each of us had forty pounds of supplies on his back. We had nothing to guide us except the distant mountains and old Jorge del Silvestra's map. I hate deserts. . . .

The pebble-strewn sands and karoo bushes stretched on forever. We marched through the cool evenings. Then we slept in what little shade we could find during the broiling-hot days. And with every step, our precious water supply shrank.

At last we found water. The place was marked on old del Silvestra's map as an oasis. But it was only a still, bad-tasting pool hidden among some rocks. We gulped down the warm water without looking too closely at it.

As the sun rose, Umbopa pointed. We saw our goal, rising out of the Suliman Mountains: the majestic volcanoes called the twin peaks of Sheba.

We dragged on. We reached the base of the mountains and began to climb. Both volcanoes seemed ancient and dead, and little grew there. We climbed for an exhausting week. At the end of it, though, we reached a high, cool, grassy pass where wild melons grew. We feasted on them. That night, after nearly baking to death for so long on the desert, we nearly froze to death as icy winds began to whistle through the high pass.

Finally, one morning, I sat panting between Sir Henry, Captain Good, and Umbopa. Our backs were to the desert we had walked across, and we sat facing a valley. I stared out across miles of beautiful landscape. It lay before us like a map. In one place there was thick forest; in another, a great river wound its silvery way through undisturbed countryside. To the left stretched a large area of rich, rolling veldt, or grassland. On it we could just barely see countless herds of game or cattle. It was a rich reward for all our suffering.

Sir Henry shaded his eyes as he peered into the valley. "Isn't there something on the map about Solomon's Great Road?"

I nodded. "Yes. We haven't found a trace of it, though."

"We have now. There it is," Sir Henry said, pointing in the distance. There on the plain was what looked like a wide highway, similar to a Roman road. It led into the distance. We climbed down to it as fast as we could. We found a splendid road cut out of the solid rock, at least fifty feet wide. It seemed to be in good condition. The really odd thing about it was that it began at the base of one of the twin peaks of Sheba.

Sir Henry said, "It runs right into the solid mountain. What do you make of that, Quatermain?"

I scratched my ear with my right leg—as I often did when I was thinking—but before I could answer, Captain Good snapped his fingers. "I have it! The road ran right over the mountain range. Then it continued across the desert to the other side, but the sand of the desert has covered it up. There at the base of the mountain range, the road has been covered by the volcano, by molten lava!"

I stopped scratching. "You must be right," I said, admiring the captain's intelligence. We set off down the road into the heart of this valley. I had never seen such amazing engineering. At one point, a magnificent stone bridge led across a deep ravine. Later, a tunnel cut from solid rock took the road through thirty yards of granite. The sides of the tunnel were decorated with stone sculptures, mostly of soldiers in armor, driving chariots.

Sir Henry looked at these. "The map may call this Solomon's Great Road, but my personal opinion is that the Egyptians built it, not Solomon. That's Egyptian stonework."

Though travel had become easier, we were all tired. We rested near a stream just off the side of the road. Ferns and wild asparagus overgrew its banks. The soft air murmured through the leaves of the silver trees, doves sang, and colorful birds flashed like living gems from branch to branch. It was like Paradise.

I turned around and around in a clump of ferns.

Finally, when I had pounded them down just right, I lay on my stomach, relaxing. Sir Henry and Umbopa sat talking. But where was Captain Good?

I lifted my head and took a good sniff. What was that smell? Soap? In the middle of nowhere? I looked up from my soft bed of ferns and saw the captain. I had noticed what a tidy man he was. He was standing by the stream, wearing nothing but his flannel shirt and boots. He stared hard into a small mirror and started to shave. It was not easy—there was no hot water, and he had a heavy beard. I was listening to the razor's scraping when, suddenly, a bright flash of metal zipped by his head.

I leaped to my paws and spun around. There, not twenty paces from us, was a group of men. They were very tall, like Zulus, but copper-colored. Some of them wore great plumes of black feathers on their heads. A few wore short cloaks of leopard skins.

A handsome youth of about seventeen stood in front of the group. His right arm was still moving. I realized he had just thrown a knife at Captain Good and missed. An older man stepped forward, said something to the youth, and they all moved toward us.

Sir Henry, Good, and Umbopa grabbed their rifles and lifted them, ready to frighten the strangers.

"Don't!" I barked. "They don't know what rifles are!"

I trotted up to the gray-haired old man, wagging my tail for all I was worth.

"Greetings," I said in Zulu. To my great surprise, he understood me.

"Greetings," answered the man. "Where did you come from? What are you? And why are the faces of three of you white, and the face of the fourth is as the faces of our mothers' sons?"

I said, "We are strangers and come in peace."

"You lie," he answered. "No strangers can cross the mountains where all things die. But even if you are strangers, you must die, for it is the king's law."

"What did he say?" asked Good.

Still trying to look friendly, I said softly, "He says they're going to kill us."

"Then I'm going to clean my teeth first," he said. He took out his false teeth, rinsed them in the stream, then placed them back into his mouth. The threatening warriors together let out a loud yell of horror as they jumped back.

"His teeth startled them," whispered Sir Henry excitedly. "Take them out again, Good." Captain Good quickly popped them out of his mouth and dropped them into his shirt pocket.

Soon the old man stepped forward. "How is it, O strangers, that this man's teeth come out and go in? Why does the hair grow on one side of his face but not the other? And why does he have one shining eye?"

"Captain Good, would you please open your mouth?" I asked. The captain quickly grinned widely. The warriors gasped when they saw his pink gums.

The old man asked, "Where are his teeth? With our eyes we saw them!"

Good moved his hands across his mouth. Then he grinned again, and there were two rows of perfect teeth.

The young man fell to the ground with a howl of terror. The old man trembled.

"I see that you are spirits," the old man said with hesitation. "Excuse us, O my lords."

"Should I take out my monocle?" Good whispered out of the side of his mouth.

"I don't think that will be necessary," I said out of the side of mine. I turned back to the old man. "You are excused," I said, thinking fast. "We . . . uh . . . come from another world, though we are men such as you. We come . . . uh . . . from the biggest star that shines at night. We have come to stay with you a little while and . . . uh . . . bless you. My friend is the . . . uh . . . Chief Sorcerer of the Pale Pop-Apart People. You will see, O friends, that I have prepared myself by learning your language."

"Only, my lord," said the old man, "you have learned it very badly."

I started to growl at him, but then I thought better of it. I said, "Now, you might think that after so long a journey, we might strike down the one who threw a knife at the head of him whose teeth come and go."

"Spare him, my lords!" the old man cried. "He is the king's son. I am his uncle."

I waved my paw grandly. "We will spare him. But just so you will not doubt our power, I will show you the magic tube that speaks."

I wagged my tail at Umbopa, who handed me my repeating rifle. Looking around for wild game, I spotted just the thing. I pointed at a small antelope standing on a rock outcropping a little more than seventy yards away.

I said, "Tell me, is it possible to kill that beast from here, with only a noise?"

The old man said, "It is not possible, my lord."

"Still, I will do it." I took aim carefully, shot, and the antelope went down. A groan of terror burst from the group in front of us.

"If you yet doubt our power," I went on, "let one of you go stand upon that rock. I will do the same to him as I have done to that buck."

None of them wanted to try. After a moment, the king's son spoke.

"Uncle, go stand upon the rock. It is but a buck that the magic has killed. Surely it cannot kill a man."

"No!" the old man cried, as he looked at his group. "My old eyes have seen enough. These are spirits or wizards, indeed. Let us bring them to the king. If any of you would wish further proof of the powers of these beings, let him stand upon the rock, so that the magic tube may speak to him."

No one came forward.

The old man turned back to us. "Listen, children of the stars, who roar out in thunder and kill from afar. I am Infadoos, son of Kafa, once king of the Kukuana people. This youth is Scragga."

"What a name," murmured Good.

"Well," I whispered back, "he nearly scragged . . . I mean killed *you!*"

"Scragga is the son of my half-brother Twala, the great king. Twala is husband of a thousand wives, chief and lord of the Kukuanas, keeper of the great road, terror of all his enemies, student of the magic arts, leader of a hundred thousand warriors. Twala, the One-eyed, the Terrible."

"We will speak to your king," I said. "The antelope I killed will be a feast for him. Lead us then to Twala."

"The way is long. We are hunting three days away from where the king lives. But let my lords have patience and we shall lead them."

The Kukuanas at once picked up everything we had. They were ready to carry our equipment for us. They even picked up Good's pants before he could put them on.

When he tried to get them back, the old man shook his head. "No, my lord," said Infadoos. "Would my lord cover up his beautiful white legs from the eyes of his servants?"

"Henry!" Good cried. "That man has my trousers!"

"Look here, Good," said Sir Henry. "I'm sorry, but you impressed them just the way you are. I'm afraid you're stuck with a flannel shirt, a pair of boots, and an eyeglass."

"Yes," I added, wagging my tail and trying not to laugh. "And you didn't finish shaving. You've made them think the whiskers grow on only one side of your face. If you change anything, the Kukuanas will feel we tricked them. They'll kill us for sure."

"Do you really think so?" Good asked gloomily.

I nodded. "I do, indeed. Your teeth, your 'beautiful white legs,' and your eyeglass have saved us. But at least you still have your boots—and you won't miss your trousers too much. It's a warm day!"

Allan Quatermain learned that adventure gets you into some very uncomfortable places! Of course, you can't have adventures without a little discomfort.

On the other hand, I always like to be comfortable—and there's a perfect spot for comfort where the morning sun comes in and makes a nice, warm place on the smooth floor of the Henderson Memorial Public Library!

Chapter Four

In the library, Wishbone lay in his spot of sunlight, stretched, and yawned. Dogs weren't usually allowed in the library. But the previous summer, Wishbone had been given permission by Joe's mom, the reference librarian, to go inside as long as no one complained. Joe, Sam, and David were doing research on Willow Bend. *Too bad so many other kids had the same idea,* Wishbone thought, as he looked around.

Joe carried a huge, dusty volume over to the table where David and Sam were reading documents on local history. He dropped his book down and said, "I got the atlas of old maps."

Wishbone's nose twitched as he got a whiff of the dusty, strangely spicy scent of the old book. He thought about getting up and taking a look at the maps. Then he thought about how the sun was just exactly warm enough where he was. Besides, once the kids made their plans, he'd find out where they were going. He stretched and yawned again.

I'd better gather my strength for the journey, he thought. He shifted a bit, putting his head on his paws.

Above him, he heard a dry, crackling sound as Joe carefully turned the large pages of the old atlas. "Here we are," he said. "This map is over a hundred years old. Let's see. . . . Here's Oakdale."

David took a small notepad from the pocket of his blue-and-white-striped sport shirt. He used his pen to make a couple of marks on it. "According to the legend on this map, an inch equals two miles. Let's see where the map places Willow Bend and how far it is from Oakdale."

"Here's Willow Bend," Sam said, putting her finger on the map. She was wearing her red baseball cap. She bent over so far that the bill of the cap almost touched the page. "There's not much detail here, is there? Guys, this is a pretty sketchy map. I'm sure in the past ten years other kids have seen it. I don't think it's too accurate."

David measured carefully. "Hmm . . . it's not quite seven miles from Oakdale. As the crow flies, that is."

Wishbone looked up. "Crow? Crow? There's a crow in here?"

"It may be seven miles in a straight line, but it'll be closer to nine miles by bike," Joe said. "A good, long ride. Are you up for it?"

"Sure," Sam said. "Hey, here's something interesting." She held up the book she had been reading. "This local history book says that one of the biggest families to move from Willow Bend to Oakdale after the flood was that of Jebediah Barnes. He could have been one of your ancestors, David."

"Could be," David said, making notes on his pad.

Joe bent over the map. "Sam, you may be right about the map not being accurate. Some hills, a few rivers, and a few roads, and that's about it. Everything I've heard says that Willow Bend was located in a big loop of the Willow River. This map shows the Willow River, all right. But the spot marked 'Willow Bend' is on a pretty straight part. See? Hardly a curve at all."

Sam read the date of the map. "Well, this map was made the year of the flood. Maybe the river changed course or something. Or maybe the map was drawn sometime *after* the flood, and no one was exactly sure where the town was anymore."

"Here's a big bend in the river," David said, pointing. "Almost a horseshoe curve. It's about two miles away from the point marked 'Willow Bend.' But it's actually closer to Oakdale. About five miles from town. Want to check that out first?"

"Sure," Joe said. "If the spot labeled 'Willow Bend' really is on the wrong part of the river, that may be why nobody's found the cornerstone yet."

Ellen Talbot walked toward him, carrying a bulging file folder. "Here comes your mom. What does she have?" Sam asked.

Wishbone glanced around. Joe's mom looked very professional in her white blouse and gray skirt. "This may help," Ellen said, placing the folder onto the table. "I don't think anyone's looked at these yet."

Joe opened the file. "What is it? Photos?"

Wishbone got up and stretched to see. Joe held up an eight-by-ten-inch photo. It was in black-and-white, and it didn't look like much of anything. It was just fuzzy bits of lighter and darker grays.

"Aerial photos," Ellen said. "They're from the U.S. Geological Survey pictures of the area around Oakdale. Many years ago, the government tried to take photos of the whole country from airplanes. This set is more than ten years old, but it shows everything for miles around."

"Hey," David said, pulling a picture out of the stack. "Look at this! I can see my house!"

"And there's ours," Joe said. "Neat!"

Ellen smiled. "The pictures are numbered on the back, and there's a map that shows you how they cover the area. Be sure to put them back in the right order."

"Sure, Mom," Joe said. He pulled out a small map that had been marked off in numbered rectangles. "Thanks."

Joe supervised, reading from the map as David and Sam laid the photos out on the table. Before long they had covered the whole tabletop. They had put together a photographic survey of everything from Oakdale to the Willow River.

"Look at this," David said. "This is the Moonlight Drive-In Theater."

"Here's my house," Sam said, pointing at another photo.

Wishbone jumped up into a chair. "Where's my doggie door? Oh, and does it show Wanda's yard? Hey, Joe, I want to see!"

"Off the chair, Wishbone," Joe said, picking him up and gently putting him on the floor.

David had come around to the other side of the table. "Weird," he said. "Look at this. There's no bend where there should be a bend."

Joe looked at the photo. "You're right," he said. "There's just that sort of curved pond off to one side of the river."

Wishbone looked up. "I want to see! Let me see! Will someone please listen to the dog?"

Sam noticed him and laughed. She held up the photo. "Is this what you want, boy?"

Wishbone sat down, all attention. "Yes! Thanks, Sam!" He stared at the photo. A curvy black line. *That must be the Willow River,* Wishbone thought. The line

wound up the left edge of the photo. Close to the top, a black crescent, like the shape of a horseshoe, stood off to the right of the river. The crescent was a curved pond.

Joe took the photo from Sam and studied it. "I'll bet I know what happened. The river had a big bend in it. Then the current cut through the neck of the bend, right here. See? That cut off the curve. So it became a pond instead of part of the river."

Sam looked over his shoulder. "That's a farmhouse there. See the barn? And the plowed fields? All the land around there looks like farms."

David had opened a modern atlas, and he leafed through until he found the map he was looking for. "Joe, I think you're right. On this map, that curved pond is called Half Moon Lake. It's about five miles out of town."

"That's not too far," Joe said. "Why don't we ride our bikes out there and look around?"

Wishbone's ears perked right up. "Great idea, Joe! It's a warm, sunny morning, and a run in the country is just what this dog would love! We can get close to nature. We can dig up the past. Running and digging are two of my favorite hobbies. I'm ready when you are."

Sam began to stack the photos. "Let's get these back in order, and then we'll go exploring," she said.

Wishbone walked back and forth impatiently. When the photos had been replaced in their folder, Joe took them over to his mom at the reference desk. "Thanks, Mom," he said. "We're going to go check out some possibilities."

"Don't go onto anyone's property without asking," Ellen said. She took the folder and added, "But I don't think that will be a problem. Everyone around Oakdale is used to this annual cornerstone hunt by now. But do remember to ask."

"We will," Joe said. He went back to the table and grabbed his backpack. Sam and David picked theirs up, too. Wishbone followed his three friends outside.

He practically danced as the kids climbed onto their bikes. "Which way are we going? Tell me, and I'll lead the way. Straight into adventure. Let's go! What are we waiting for—guys?"

Wishbone looked around. Joe, Sam, and David had rolled away, heading south on Oak Street. They were pedaling past Snook's Furniture. Wishbone ran after them as fast as his four legs could carry him.

"Guys! Hey, guys! You're leaving your trusty guide behind! Helllooo!" Wishbone ran after his friends, his ears flapping in the breeze. This was just what he needed. Fun, excitement, and a search for something that had been missing for a long, long time.

We're off on a quest! Who knows what dangers may lurk along our path? What kind of excitement might we find as we make our way forward? As Allan Quatermain knew, you never can tell when you're on an adventure like this!

Chapter Five

All that afternoon we followed Solomon's Great Road. It led us northwest. The gray-haired Infadoos and the scowling Scragga walked with us, but their followers marched about one hundred yards ahead.

"Infadoos," I asked, "who built this road?"

He gave me a puzzled glance. He probably wondered why the magicians from the stars didn't know that. He said, "It was made, my lord, in the old time. No one knows how or when. Not even the wise woman, Gagool the Old, knows, and she has lived for generations. The road was here when the Kukuanas came into this land from the hills beyond like the breath of a storm. That was ten thousand moons ago. The country was good, so we settled here and grew strong until our numbers became as great as the grains of sand in the desert, far beyond counting."

As we marched along the magnificent road, Infadoos told us of the recent history of the Kukuanas and the rise of King Twala. His story made me feel itchy, as if I needed a good flea bath.

He explained: "Twala the king was the weak twin of

my half-brother, Imotu. Everyone thought Twala had died as a baby. But he was hidden away not long after his birth by Gagool. When a famine came upon the land, Gagool brought Twala out of his hiding place. By then he was a grown man. She showed everyone where the tattoo of the sacred snake wrapped around his waist and cried aloud, 'Behold your king, whom I have saved for you even to this day! He will end the famine!' And the people, mad as starving lions with hunger, cried out, 'The king! The king!'"

"What about your half-brother, Imotu, the real king?" I asked.

Infadoos shook his gray head and looked grim. "When Imotu, the king, heard Gagool, he came forth. At once his twin, Twala, stabbed him through the heart with his knife. He did so in front of the eyes of his brother's wife and his three-year-old son, Ignosi."

Something itched in my memory then, something I could not quite scratch. I asked, "Did Twala slay them, as well?"

With a sigh, Infadoos replied, "She and the child disappeared that night. My people think they died in the dark mountains, running to get far away from the new king's anger."

I translated for my friends, and Sir Henry looked shocked. "Then if this child Ignosi had lived, he would be the true king of the Kukuana people?" he asked. I translated the question for Infadoos.

Infadoos nodded. "This is so, my lord. The sacred snake tattoo is also round his middle. If he lived, he would be the king. But alas. He surely is long dead."

When I told Sir Henry, he, too nodded. I found my ears pricking up as I watched Umbopa. He had been listening to our conversation with Infadoos. The expression on his face made me think of a man struggling to remember something long forgotten. When he noticed me, he quickly turned away. *This man has more secrets to tell us,* I thought, but I did not ask about them then.

Infadoos had sent a runner ahead to notify the village of our arrival. We soon came within sight of the huge circular fence, cattle pens, and grass-covered huts that made up the kraal, or village. When we arrived, a welcoming committee waited in front of its gates. By the time we came to the slope, an army of tall warriors had marched out and had taken up their positions along the road.

They were all mature, strong men. Not one of them stood under six feet tall. They wore heavy black Sacaboola plumes on their heads and around their waists. Around their right knees, they had tied circles of white ox tails. In their left hands, they held round shields

made of thin iron and milk-white ox hide. In their right hands, they carried assegais, short and very heavy two-edged spears on wooden shafts, with iron tips.

Sir Henry placed his hand upon my shoulder as he stared at the gathered men. "I say, Quatermain, it looks like a warm reception."

"Let not my lords be afraid," said Infadoos quickly. "My soldiers will not attack you. These warriors are under my command, and they come by my orders to greet you."

I realized that the Kukuanas, like the Zulu people, were very advanced in warfare. Both groups organized their armies into what Europeans would refer to as "regiments." Each regiment had at least a thousand warriors, and perhaps three times that many. I estimated that the gray-haired, wrinkle-faced Infadoos commanded a regiment of about thirty-six hundred.

Luckily, they did seem peaceful. We marched between their ranks and into the kraal. And what a kraal it was! It was at least a mile around. A dry moat, an empty ditch ten feet deep, surrounded it. Inside that was a palisade, a strong wall made of upright tree trunks, sharpened at the top ends. The only way across the moat and through the gate was across a drawbridge that could be raised by rawhide ropes.

Inside the fence, we saw cattle pens. Beyond them were the huts of the villagers. These looked much like Zulu huts. They were built on a strong framework of flexible twigs, and they were covered with bunches of grass. Near the center of the kraal, Infadoos stopped at the door of a large hut and motioned us to go in.

"Enter, sons of the stars, and rest. My servants will bring food so that you shall have no need to tighten your belts from hunger. You will have some honey and some milk and an ox or two, and a few sheep. It is not much, my lords, but still a little food will refresh you."

"It is good," I said, my mouth watering. "Infadoos, we are tired from traveling from the stars. Now let us rest, and then we will eat."

Later that night, we took part of Infadoos's "little food." It was a royal feast, a banquet. The Kukuanas killed several oxen for us. We made many friends when we returned nearly all of the meat to the warriors and their families.

Later, Infadoos and Scragga joined us in our hut. We talked throughout the night. The old man was friendly and polite, but the young prince eyed us with suspicion. It seemed to me that when Scragga saw we ate, drank, and slept like other humans, he suspected we were just men, like himself. That probably made him angry. I don't think he liked being tricked by stories of sorcerers from the stars.

But Infadoos still seemed to be our friend. With the light of an oil lamp gleaming on his gray hair and wrinkled face, he spoke for a long time. He told us that Twala was in his great kraal, named Loo. We would be traveling there. It was only two days' march away. The king was preparing for the great annual feast. It was a time when all the troops paraded before him, and the great annual witch-hunt was held.

"Witch-hunt?" Captain Good asked, his right eye wide with suspicion behind its monocle. I thought he was hoping his false teeth wouldn't lead the Kukuanas to believe he was a witch. "What is that?"

"Gagool finds men she says are witches," Infadoos said slowly. "And they—"

"They will see when we get there," Scragga said harshly.

I swallowed hard. I had no wish to see a witch hunt. But it seemed I had no choice.

We got an early start and followed Solomon's Great Road into the heart of Kukuanaland. Infadoos's soldiers marched as our escort. As we made our way, the countryside grew richer. The kraals, with their surrounding farms, became more and more numerous. Our band of soldiers soon joined others. Thousands of warriors were hurrying up to Loo to the annual gathering. Despite Infadoos's guarantees of safety, I was nervous. I told Sir Henry and Captain Good to keep their rifles ready for trouble.

At sunset of the second day, we stopped to rest upon some hills overlooking a fertile plain. We could see Loo itself. It was an enormous place, easily five miles around. It was located in front of an odd horseshoe-shaped hill. A small river ran right through the kraal, dividing it into two parts. Sixty or seventy miles off, three great purple snow-capped mountains rose from the level yellow plain. Infadoos pointed at them. "The Great Road ends there, my lords, in the midst of the mountains we call 'the Three Witches.'"

"Why does it end?" I asked, casually scratching my ear with my thoughtful leg.

"Who knows?" he answered with a shrug. "The mountains are full of caves, and there is a great pit between them. In the old times, the wise men used to go there to get whatever it was they came to this country for. Now our kings of old rest there forever." Then he looked at us sharply. "But surely my lords who come from the stars know this."

I stopped scratching. "Oh, sure! We from the stars know many things. Uh . . . for instance, we know that these wise men came to those mountains to get bright stones and the . . . uh . . . yellow iron."

"My lord is wise," he said calmly. "I am but a child and cannot talk with my lord of such things. My lord must speak with Gagool the Old, at the king's palace. She knows many things."

Then Infadoos turned away.

Oops, sore subject, I thought, as I trotted back to the rest of my group. But I knew something now I hadn't known before. If ancient people had taken yellow gold and shining diamonds from the place where the road ended, that meant just one thing. I sat next to Sir Henry and pointed at the Three Witches. "Those mountains guard King Solomon's mines."

Captain Good, still in his flannel shirt, boots, and without pants—and still not happy about it—shaded his eyes with his hands and squinted. "Are you sure, Quatermain? I mean, how can you tell?"

Behind us, Umbopa laughed his deep, booming laugh. We all turned to him.

"Macumazahn speaks the truth, my lords," he rumbled, nodding at me. "The diamonds are surely there, and you shall have them. You men are like children, fond of toys."

"How do you know where the diamonds are, Umbopa?" I asked sharply. Sometimes the man was just too mysterious for comfort.

He laughed again. "I dreamed it in the night." Then he, too, turned on his heel and left us.

"Now, what was that all about?" asked Sir Henry, thoughtfully stroking his blond beard. "He knows more than he's telling us, that much is for sure. But has he heard anything of my brother?"

Sir Henry knew that Umbopa had my instructions to ask the Kukuanas about George Curtis. I shook my head and said, "So far, everyone Umbopa has spoken to has said that no white man has been seen in the area for hundreds of years."

"Do you suppose he ever got here at all?" asked Good, polishing his monocle. "We ourselves have only reached the place by a miracle."

"I don't know," Sir Henry said gloomily. "But somehow, I have a feeling that I shall find him."

I hope you're right, Sir Henry, I thought. *I truly hope you're right.*

The ox pens of the king of the Kukuanas covered six or seven acres in the center of Loo. Around the outside of the circular pen fence was a row of huts. They were the homes of the king's many wives. Opposite the gateway, on the far side of a wide-open space, was a very large hut. The king lived there. The four of us stood in the hot sun with thousands of Kukuana warriors who had gathered. We all waited. Not even lords from the stars, I thought, panting, could rush a king.

After a while, the door of the hut opened. A huge figure with a splendid leopard skin over his shoulders stepped out. He was followed by the boy, Scragga, and a dried-up being who crept on all fours. But not one of us looked at the two. All eyes were on the giant.

He was a muscular man, and he looked cruel. He had only one eye, and it gleamed black. The other eye socket was sunken and hollow. From his head rose a magnificent crown of white ostrich feathers. His body was covered in a shirt of shining, heavy chain mail. Around his neck, he wore a thick circle of gold. Tied securely to his forehead on a leather cord was a single enormous diamond.

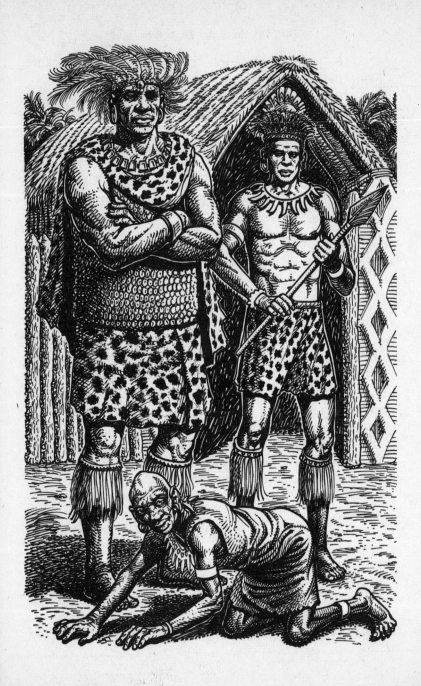

"Be humble, O people," said a thin voice. It came from the dried-up, creeping shape. "It is the king."

"It is the king!" boomed eight thousand voices in answer. The silence that followed was broken only by the sound of a spear falling. The eye of Twala the king quickly spotted the young warrior who had dropped his weapon.

"Scragga, my son," the king rumbled, "let me see how well you can use your sharp spear. Kill this awkward fool for me."

With an evil grin, the boy stepped forward and hurled his spear. It struck the young warrior. He fell dead. He had been hit so hard that the spear stuck out a foot beyond his back.

"The king's word has been spoken," whispered the withered thing. "The king's doom is done."

Sir Henry boiled with rage at what had just happened. "That was murder!" he exclaimed. "Cold-blooded murder!"

I put a paw on his leg. "Yes, it was. Now sit down, for heaven's sake," I whispered. "Our lives depend on it."

The cruel eye of the king aimed toward us. "I hear you speak with a loud voice, people of the stars. Remember that the stars are far off, and you are here. Should I make you as him who my son has slain?"

Scragga reached for another spear and lifted it high over his shoulder.

Oh, this is bad, I thought. *This is really bad.* I leaned toward Sir Henry, who sat with his rifle across his lap. "Sir Henry," I whispered. "You think you can shoot the blade off Scragga's spear?"

"With pleasure," he said. Immediately, he raised the rifle and fired. The tip of the spear exploded from the shaft. With a scream, Scragga dropped the shaft and ran back into the hut. Twala did not move at all, but the withered figure did.

It rose to its feet. It was a bald woman of great age, so shrunken in size she was hardly larger than a four-year-old child. She might have been taken for a sun-dried corpse, except for her eyes. They were large, black, and full of fire and intelligence.

Suddenly, she pointed a long finger at us and screamed. "Listen, O King! Listen, O people! Listen, O mountains and plains and rivers, home of the Kukuana race! The spirit of life is in me, and I foresee doom!"

The words faded away in a faint wail. Terror seemed to overtake all who heard them. I know *I* felt terror!

She waved her arms and screeched, "Blood! Blood! Blood! Rivers of blood—blood everywhere. I see it, I smell it, I taste it—it is salt. It runs red upon the ground. The lions shall lap it up and roar! The vultures shall wash their wings in it and cry in joy!"

Then she turned her bald head toward us. She looked like a vulture herself.

"What do you seek, white men of the stars? Do you seek a lost one? You shall never find him here. Never for ages has a white foot pressed upon this land. You come for the bright stones. I know! You shall find them when the blood is dry if you stand with me!"

"She's very creepy," I whispered out of the corner of my muzzle. Sir Henry and Captain Good nodded in agreement as she turned toward Umbopa.

"And you—with the dark skin and proud posture— who are you, and what do you seek? Not stones that shine, not yellow metal that gleams. I almost know you. I can almost smell the scent of the blood in your veins!"

Then Gagool fell to the ground. She moaned and foamed at the mouth. Two warriors came and carried her back inside the hut. The king waved his hand and the soldiers marched away. We were left alone with the monstrous Twala.

"Strangers, it is in my mind to kill you, for Gagool has spoken strange words. But I will not. Tonight is the great dance. You shall see it. Fear not that I shall set a trap for you. Tomorrow, I shall think what to do with you."

I stood. "We magicians from the stars will look kindly on you for your hospitality, O King. It is well." *Is he buying any of this?* I wondered. *I think so. . . . Well, I hope he's buying this.*

When we reached the hut that had been set aside for us, I motioned to Infadoos to enter, too.

"Infadoos," I said, "your king is a cruel man."

Infadoos looked at the ground. "It is so, my lords. The very land cries out with his cruelties! Tonight is the great witch-hunt. Many will be smelled out by Gagool as witches and will be killed. No man is safe. Many will die before the stars grow pale. The land groans under the cruelties of Twala the king. It is tired of him and his bloody ways."

"Then why do the people not kill him?" I growled, the fur on my neck rising.

Infadoos leaned close and lowered his voice. "If Twala were slain, then Scragga would rule in his place. The heart of Scragga is even more cruel than that of his father! If my half-brother, Imotu, or his son, Ignosi, had lived, it would have been otherwise. Alas, they are both dead."

"How do you know that Ignosi is dead?" asked a voice behind us. I looked around in surprise to see who spoke. It was Umbopa.

"What do you mean, child?" asked Infadoos, sounding angry. "We are two elders talking of serious matters. Who told you to speak?"

Umbopa held his head high. "Listen, Infadoos," he said, "and I will tell you a story. Years ago, King Imotu was killed, and his wife fled from your land with the boy, Ignosi. Is it not so?"

"It is so."

"It was said that the woman and the boy died upon the mountains. Is it not so?"

"It is so."

"Well, they did not die. They crossed the mountains and the deserts until they came to fresh water and green grass again."

"How do you know?" Infadoos asked in disbelief.

Umbopa's eyes flashed. "I know, Infadoos, I know. Years passed. The mother died. The son wandered until he met some white men who searched for one who is lost. They crossed the burning desert, they crossed the snow-covered mountains. They reached the land of the Kukuanas, and there they met you, O Infadoos."

Infadoos stared at Umbopa. "Surely you are insane to talk like this!"

"What are they talking about?" Captain Good asked me, unable to follow their language.

I lifted a paw. "Shh! I'll tell you in a minute."

Umbopa had paid no attention to us. He said, "You think I am insane? I will show you who I am, O my uncle. I am Ignosi, rightful king of the Kukuanas!"

With that, he tore off his shirt and pointed to his waist. Around it was tattooed a great blue snake, its tail disappearing into its open mouth. Infadoos gazed, his eyes wide. Then he fell to his knees.

"You are Imotu's son!" he cried. "You are the king! I

65

put my hands between your hands! I am your servant until death!"

Sir Henry and Captain Good both elbowed me. I tried to explain quickly. "Umbopa isn't Umbopa. He's Ignosi, king of the Kukuanas!"

"This might mean trouble," Captain Good said.

"I'll say," I agreed. "I'm not sure we can afford to pay his salary if he's a king!"

Umbopa—or rather Ignosi—turned and smiled at me. He said in English, "You owe me nothing, Mr. Quatermain, for you brought me home. Now, will you and your friends help me? I offer you the shining stones. If I conquer the kingdom and you find the diamonds, you shall have as many as you can carry."

Sir Henry stood tall and looked him in the eye. "I have always liked my friend Umbopa. I do not like him less as Ignosi the king. I will stand by you in this business. What say you, Good?"

"I will say the same," Good replied with a laugh. "I've always liked a good fight. As long as I get to do it in trousers!"

"And what say you, Macumazahn?" Ignosi said to me. "Are you, too, with me, old hunter, more clever than a wounded buffalo?"

I scratched my head with my hind leg and sighed. "Ignosi, I don't like revolutions. I'm a man of peace. But I do stick by my friends. And, being a poor man, I will take your diamonds if you will help us in our search for Sir Henry's brother."

In the language of the Kukuanas, Ignosi said, "That I will promise. Infadoos, you are the eldest and wisest man here. Has any white man to your knowledge set his foot within the land?"

Infadoos shook his gray head. "None, O Ignosi,

until your friends came here. I have heard of such men only in old, old legends."

Sir Henry sighed. "Well," he said, "there it is. I suppose George never got here. Poor fellow. So it has all been for nothing. God's will has been done."

But maybe it hasn't been for nothing, I thought, as we sat in that great hut and began to plan how to bring down a tyrant and raise up the true king.

Chapter Six

The rest of the day we spent quietly resting and talking over the situation. Everything was getting so complicated. I hate complications. Infadoos left us alone for hours. At last he returned with some warriors, carrying three heavy bundles.

"These are war shirts from the old times," Infadoos explained. "You each must wear one."

I opened a bundle and took out a chain-mail shirt. It was armor made of linked rings of metal.

"Steel?" Sir Henry asked, taking another one out. "It looks ancient, and yet it is bright and shining."

"The ancient people made these," Infadoos said. "We have hardly a dozen left. They will protect us against any blade."

Sir Henry Curtis was our expert on ancient times.

"Is this Egyptian armor?" I asked him.

"No," Sir Henry said slowly, as he held up one of the heavy mail shirts. "I have never seen anything quite like this. Israelite, perhaps? Assyrian? Or even more ancient—thousands of years old, surely."

Infadoos said, "These shirts were left by the ancient

people who dug up the shining stones. We do not know the secret of making them. Now only our bravest warriors are allowed to wear them into battle."

"Then, Infadoos, you do us a great honor," I said. I took off my hunting jacket and slipped into one of the chain-mail shirts. It was quite heavy, but I was glad for its protection. Then I put my jacket back on. No one could tell I was wearing a spear-proof vest underneath. Captain Good and Sir Henry got into theirs, too. Good also had his trousers on.

Then Infadoos said, "Come. The Great Dance is about to begin."

It was a dark, moonless night. The kraal was closely packed with at least twenty thousand men. Each troop was separated by a little path. The paths allowed the witch-finders to move among them, Infadoos told us in a whisper. They stood perfectly silent, torches flickering their light on a forest of raised spears.

"They are very quiet," said Good.

Infadoos replied grimly, "Those over whom the shadow of death hovers are always silent."

"Tell me," I asked Infadoos, "are we in danger?"

"I know not, my lords—I think not. But do not be afraid. If you live through the night, all may go well. The soldiers are angry with the king."

At those words, Twala—along with Scragga, his son, and Gagool the Old—appeared. The king looked at us and then sat in his throne. He smiled. At least I think it was a smile—his lips moved, anyway.

"Greetings, white lords!" he cried. "Let us not waste precious time. The night is all too short for the deeds that must be done. Look around, white lords, look around!" He rolled his one wicked eye from regiment to regiment. "See how they shake in fear, all those who have evil in their hearts and who dread the judgment of Twala!"

"Begin!" cried out Gagool in her thin, piercing voice. "The hyenas are hungry. They howl for food! Begin! Begin!"

Instantly, strange and awful figures came running. Their bare feet pattered on the hard-packed earth. They were ten old women, their white hair streaming out behind them. Their faces were painted in stripes of white and yellow. Down their backs hung snakeskins, and around their waists rattled belts of human bones. They stopped in front of Gagool, who smiled at them.

"Are your eyes sharp, you seers in dark places?" she said in a shrill voice, loud after the silence.

"Mother, they are sharp!"

"Good! Good! Good! Can you smell blood? Can you rid the land of the wicked ones who plot evil against the king? Then go! Wait not, you vultures, the king's executioners make sharp their spears! Go!"

"Mother, we go!"

With a bloodcurdling yell, the weird group broke away in every direction. The dry bones around their waists rattled as they scattered. One old woman came our way. She halted in front of a group of soldiers and began to dance wildly.

"I smell the evil-doer!" she shrieked. "He is near, a man who thought evil of the king!"

With a cry, she sprang in and touched a tall warrior. Instantly, the men on either side of the warrior grabbed the doomed man and dragged him toward the king.

"Kill!" said the king.

"Kill!" squeaked Gagool.

"Kill!" echoed Scragga, with a hollow chuckle.

Almost before the words were said, the horrible

deed was done. One of the executioners drove his spear through the man's heart.

"One," counted Twala the king.

This had hardly been done before the guards dragged up another poor soul. He seemed like an ox brought to the slaughter. Again the awful words were spoken, and the victim fell dead.

"Two," counted Twala the king.

The deadly game went on until more than a hundred bodies were stretched in rows in front of us. Once we tried to protest, but Twala angrily waved his arm and ordered us to be silent.

He roared, "Let my law take its course, white men. These are magicians and evil-doers. It is my decision they all should die."

Another man was brought forward and killed.

"One hundred and three," counted Twala the king. And Gagool the Old herself came dancing toward us.

Good leaned toward me. "Hang me if I don't believe that she is going to try her wicked games on us!" he exclaimed in horror.

"Nonsense!" snapped Sir Henry, his rifle at the ready. All the fur along my back stood up. I growled in spite of myself as the old woman danced closer and closer. At last she stood still and pointed.

"So, who's it to be?" Sir Henry muttered. Then the old woman rushed toward us and touched Ignosi on the shoulder.

"I smell him out!" she cried. "Kill him! Kill him! He is full of evil! Kill him, the stranger, before blood flows for him! Slay him, O King!"

Before anyone could move, I howled a warning. Thousands of pairs of eyes turned as I jumped up in front of Ignosi. "O King, this man is the friend of your guests!

By the sacred and ancient law of hospitality, I claim protection for him!"

"Gagool, mother of the witch doctors, has smelled him out," snarled the king. "He must die. Seize him!"

"Stand back!" I cried, pointing my revolver at Twala. "One move, and the king dies!" Luckily for all of us, Sir Henry and Captain Good had their rifles out and at the ready.

Twala glared at us. I was sure Scragga had told him about the guns. The king spoke at last. "Put away your magic tubes. You are our guests. For that reason, and not out of fear, I spare him."

"It is well," I said, putting away the revolver. "We are tired of the killings. Is the dance ended?"

"It is ended," Twala said. "Now let the evil-doers be thrown out to the hyenas and the vultures. Let the people rejoice."

He turned and left. In the far-off distance, drums began to pound. The thousands of warriors marched away in different directions, leaving us alone with the dead.

"Well, men," said Sir Henry, his cheeks pale above his yellow beard, "I feel sick."

"If I had any doubts about helping Ignosi before, they are gone now," I growled.

"You did well," Ignosi told me.

I snorted. "I did the only thing I could think of. My friend, you ought to be most grateful to us. Another few seconds, and Twala's warriors would have let some air into your skin."

"I am grateful," Ignosi answered. "And I shall not forget. Now, let us go to Infadoos. We have much to do."

For a long while—two hours, I should think—we sat in our hut in silence. We were too overwhelmed by the horrors we had seen to talk much. Outside, drums sounded as the Kukuanas celebrated the end of the witch-finding. At last the gray-haired Infadoos entered. He was followed by some half-dozen old and regal-looking chiefs.

He bowed low. "Greetings, my lords and Ignosi, rightful king of the Kukuanas. I have brought these men, each in command of three thousand warriors. Let them see the sacred snake around you, my king. Then they will join with you against Twala."

Ignosi once again took off his shirt and showed the tattoo around his waist.

"What do you say, chiefs?" Infadoos asked. "Will you stand by this man and help him to take his father's throne? The land cries out against Twala, and the blood

of the people flows like the rains of spring. Choose, my brothers!"

The eldest of the six men, a short, heavyset warrior, stepped forward and answered, "It is true, Infadoos, the land cries out. Yet how do we not know you would have us raise our spears for an impostor? If he is indeed the rightful king, give us a sign that all may see."

"You have the sign of the snake," I answered.

The old man shook his head seriously. "My lord, it is not enough. The snake may have been placed there at any time. Show us some true sign. We cannot move without a sign."

A sign greater than the snake? My weary head started to spin. *That tattoo goes all the way around his body, and that's not a big enough sign?* I spoke to my friends in English and explained the problem.

Captain Good tapped his monocle thoughtfully against his false teeth. Then he said, "I say, you fellows, isn't tomorrow June 4?" Sir Henry and I both looked at him as if he'd gone mad.

"Uh . . . Good, I don't think this is the time or—" Sir Henry began.

Good waved away Sir Henry's words. "Just hand me your pocket notebook, Henry. There's an almanac in the front of it, if I recall. . . . Ah!"

"Ah, what?" I asked. I began to get worried as I handed him the notebook. He thumbed through the book. I thought he had lost his wits.

Good looked up with a big grin. "It is right here in the almanac. I quote: 'June 4, total eclipse of the Sun begins at ten-oh-three Greenwich, England, time, visible in these islands, Africa,' and so on." He closed the little book in triumph. "Don't you see, my dear chaps? Visible from these islands and Africa! There's your sign, Ignosi.

Tell the chiefs you will darken the Sun tomorrow, right at noon."

With a great laugh, Ignosi turned to his uncle and the gathering of chiefs. He told them exactly that. They were very impressed. A tiny bit doubtful, but impressed. They agreed that darkening the Sun would certainly be a powerful sign.

"Then go," Ignosi commanded. "Tell the others. Let them be ready."

The old warriors left, bowing to Ignosi. When they were gone, we all breathed a sigh of relief.

"Wonderful idea, Good!" Sir Henry exclaimed, clapping his friend on the back. "But suppose the eclipse doesn't happen?"

Good stared at him through his monocle. "Then we are in a great deal of trouble. That would mean the Earth was off its orbit. Don't worry. We sailors are familiar with the Sun, Moon, and stars, you know. Eclipses always occur on time. Here, I've got it figured out. It was a bit hard without our exact position. But I figure the eclipse should begin about noon tomorrow and last till half-past one. Total darkness for, oh, five minutes or so."

"My friend," said Ignosi, "can you indeed do this wonderful thing, or were you merely speaking empty words to the men?"

I wasn't convinced about the eclipse. But neither could I let my friend down. Trying to appear confident, I said, "We can do it, Umbopa—Ignosi, I mean. If the people believe the Sky Lords can darken the Sun in your name, they'll do anything we ask."

"If you seem to darken the Sun, you will convince everyone you are the true king," Sir Henry added.

Oh, yes, I thought. *And if I had a long nose and weighed five tons, I could convince them I was an elephant!*

After a restless night's sleep, we were once again called upon by Twala the king. This time he wanted us to see the Dance of the Maidens. When we arrived back at the enclosure, a glorious sight awaited us. Gone were the massed ranks of Kukuana warriors.

In their place now stood rows of beautiful young Kukuana women. Each wore a wreath of flowers. All of them stood holding a palm leaf in one hand and a tall white lily in the other. They were all lovely. However, the same fear and terror that throbbed in the warriors the night before was present in them.

Twala, with Scragga and Gagool, stepped forward. The king raised his hand in greeting. "Welcome again, Sky Lords! If Gagool, here, had had her way, your friend would have been dead by now. It is lucky that you, too, came from the stars. Ha-ha!"

"I can kill you before you kill me, O King," was Ignosi's calm answer. "And you shall be stiff in death before my limbs stop bending."

Twala stared. "You speak too boldly, young one," he replied angrily.

Ignosi's eyes flashed. "He may well be bold who speaks the truth. The truth is a sharp spear that flies home and fails not, O King!"

Twala scowled and his one eye gleamed fiercely. But he turned from us and gestured grandly at the assembled girls. "Let the dance begin!" he roared.

The girls began to sway and dance, waving their palms and flowers. The sight was enchanting. Then a beautiful young woman sprang from the group and began to twirl and pirouette in front of us with a grace that would have put most ballet girls to shame. She fell back. Another girl took her place. Then another and another.

"Which of these maidens do you think is the fairest?" Twala asked me.

"Oh, the first," I said without thinking. The king grinned, and I felt as if my collar were too tight.

Twala raised his spear and said, "Then my mind is just as your mind. She is the fairest, and so she must die!"

"Aye, she must die!" cried Gagool. She pointed her shrunken talon of a finger to where the poor child stood, nervously shredding flower petals.

I was horrified. I asked, "Why, O King? The girl has danced well and pleased us. It would be hard to reward her art with death!"

"Stranger," said Twala the king, "if the king offer not a sacrifice of a fair girl to the old ones who sit and watch on the mountains, then he shall fall from favor, along with his family. My brother who reigned before me offered not the sacrifice. He lost his throne, and his wife and child died. Now I rule in his place! The girl must die! My word is law!"

At his gesture, the poor young woman was dragged before the king and his evil son, Scragga, who picked up his spear.

"Come, come, child," whispered Gagool the Old. "Tell us your name."

"Oh, Mother," the sobbing girl replied. "I am Foulata, of the family of Suko. Oh, Mother, why must I die? I have done nothing wrong!"

"Be comforted," said the old woman in a hateful, mocking tone. "You must die, indeed, as a sacrifice to the old ones who sit on the mountains. But be honored, for you shall die by the royal hand of the king's own son!"

With a scream, the girl turned and ran right for us

and hid behind Captain Good. She begged, "Oh, lords from the sky, protect me from these men and from Gagool!"

Twala motioned to his son, who came forward with his spear lifted.

"Let's do something," whispered Sir Henry to me. "What are we waiting for?"

"Well, right now we're waiting for the eclipse," I answered. "It's already past noon. I have had my eye on the Sun for the last half-hour, and I have never seen it look healthier."

Sir Henry drew himself up to his full towering height. His long blond hair and untrimmed beard made him look more like a fierce Viking warrior than ever. Sternly, he said, "We must risk it. Twala is losing patience."

Drat! I thought, but I had to do something. I took a deep breath and barked my loudest bark. "Stop! Come one step closer and we will put out the Sun and sink the land into darkness! You shall taste our magic!"

My threat produced an effect. Scragga stopped coming toward us, but he still stood with his spear upraised.

"Hear him, hear him!" piped Gagool. "Hear the liar who says he will put out the Sun like a torch. Let him do it and the girl shall be spared. Or he can die with her and all the others around him!"

I took out my pocket watch, not to check the time, but to look at the reflection of the Sun in its shiny steel case. To my great joy and relief, I saw that the almanac had not been mistaken. On the edge of the Sun's brilliant surface was a faint, round nick.

I put my watch into my pocket and lifted my paw somberly toward the sky. Sir Henry and Good did the same. I started quoting a line or two of R. W. Barham's

poetry from his book *The Ingoldsby Legends* in the loudest tone I could use. Sir Henry did the same with a verse from the Old Testament.

"Your turn, Good," Sir Henry said after reciting a psalm.

"Right," Captain Good said, rolling up his sleeves. He pointed toward Twala. In his finest sea-going English, he roared, "All right, you slab-sided, knot-headed, grass-combing lubber! You pitiful seasick swab! Shiver my timbers if I don't keel-haul you, you thrice-blasted son of a sea cook! I'll have your guts for garters, I will! Why, you—"

And so it went. Captain Good had been in the navy for a long time. He could curse better than any man I knew. Slowly the dark bite in the Sun's surface grew. The day began to dim. As it did, I heard a deep gasp of fear rise from the people around us. It was time to act.

I lifted a paw dramatically. "See, O King! Look, Gagool! Look, chiefs and people! The Sun grows dark before your eyes! Soon night will fall—aye, night in the noontime. You have asked for a sign! It is given to you!

Grow dark, O Sun! Take away the light. Bring the proud heart to dust and eat up the world with shadows!"

Screams went up from the terrified onlookers. The king sat still, silent and trembling. Only Gagool kept her courage.

"It will pass!" she cried. "I have seen the like before! No man can put out the light of the Sun! Lose not heart! The shadow will pass!"

"Wait and you shall see!" I yelped, hopping with excitement. "Keep it up, Good. I can't remember any more poetry. Curse away, my good fellow!"

The captain responded happily to the challenge. Never before had I the slightest idea of the extent of a naval officer's swearing powers. For ten more minutes he went on without stopping or repeating himself. Meanwhile, the dark ring crept on. Strange and unholy shadows blocked out the sunlight, and an almost frightening quiet filled the place.

"The Sun is dying! The witches have killed the Sun!" cried the boy Scragga. "We will all freeze in the dark!"

Driven by fear or fury, he lifted his spear and charged. He hurled the spear with all his might at Sir Henry's broad chest. Sir Henry dodged and fired his rifle in self-defense. The evil Scragga dropped dead at our feet.

At the sight, and mad with fear of the gathering gloom, the groups of girls broke up in confusion and ran screeching for the gateways. Even the king and Gagool were swept out of the enclosure. Soon only we and some of the chiefs that Infadoos had brought to our hut were left. The sky grew dark as could be, and a star or two glittered overhead.

"Now, chiefs," I growled, "we have given you the sign. If you are satisfied, let our battle begin! For the magic cannot be stopped—it will work for an hour!"

"Come," said Infadoos, turning to leave. He was followed by the amazed chiefs, ourselves, and the girl Foulata.

Before we had reached the gate of the kraal, the Sun disappeared completely. We stumbled on through the weird darkness.

Allan Quatermain and his friends are plunging into danger!

Joe, David, Sam, and I are about to plunge into a nice romp through the countryside. . . . Or are we, too, getting into more danger than we suspect?

Chapter Seven

A few minutes after noon that Saturday, Joe, David, and Sam parked their bikes under a shady oak tree. "Ready for lunch, buddy?" Joe asked Wishbone.

Lunch! Wishbone hadn't even thought about lunch. He wagged his tail so fast it felt as if he might take off! "You brought lunch, Joe? Great! A picnic! Count me in! What do we have?"

The three friends had stopped back at Joe's house after they finished at the library. They had packed sandwiches and juice for themselves. Joe had brought along a handy little container of kibble for Wishbone. He took the top off the container and set it down. Wishbone eagerly dug in. As he crunched happily on the dry dog food, Wishbone listened.

"So far," Joe said, "we seem to be striking out."

They had already visited a few farms. Up to that point, no one they had talked with knew the location of the Willow Bend cornerstone. Wishbone hoped his friends weren't getting discouraged.

"Well," David said between bites of his sandwich, "at least we know where Willow Bend *isn't*. Mr. Blake, the first farmer we spoke to, said that kids have searched the place on the map for years. If anything was there, someone would have found it by now."

Sam nodded and took a sip of orange juice. "Mrs. Whitney, back at the last farm, said the same thing. She said we could go down to the Willow River on her property, if we wanted to. But her husband has that whole part of their farm plowed up. No sign of a cornerstone there. If Mr. Whitney didn't find anything when he was plowing, there isn't anything to find."

The kids had bought a large-scale modern map of Oakdale and the countryside around it. They also had a copy of Wanda's official map. Joe held his sandwich in one hand and pinned the modern map to the ground with the other. A constant breeze blew the paper, making a corner of it flap.

"Well," Joe said, "we're between the place where we thought Willow Bend *might* have been and the spot the map *says* it is. According to the map, the next farm is named Willow Acres. I know the man who owns that place—it's Mr. Potts. He reads a lot, and I've run into him at the library. He's pretty friendly, and he told me about his farm once. Let's ask him what he knows."

Joe took a last bite of his sandwich and tossed the crust to Wishbone, who caught it expertly.

David and Sam laughed. They tossed Wishbone their crusts, too. Wishbone cheerfully gobbled the leftovers. Then the group was ready to set out again.

The three kids got on to their bicycles. Then they rode on a quiet country lane that had almost no traffic on it. Joe, David, and Sam pedaled along carefully in single file. Wishbone was up front, leading the way. He was really enjoying the day.

A warm Saturday, a picnic lunch, a good run in the

countryside . . . This is really the life, Wishbone thought. His nose suddenly twitched as he smelled a strange aroma. It was a different odor from those in the big towns. He took three deep sniffs. "Cows!"

Sure enough, the road curved to the left. Just around the bend was a fenced-in green pasture. In it, two dozen black-and-white cows stood munching grass. The animals looked up curiously as Wishbone and the kids passed by. One of them gave a low moo, as if in greeting. Wishbone looked ahead. A man wearing overalls and a wide-brimmed straw hat was kneeling and working at one of the fence posts, fixing a loose wire.

"Hi, Mr. Potts," Joe said, braking his bike to a stop. Sam and David came up beside him.

The man at the fence looked around. Wishbone saw he was a tall, muscular man, with a big nose and a red face. He smiled, showing a set of white teeth. "Joe Talbot! What are you doing out this way? No, don't tell me. I can guess. Miss Gilmore's got you on her cornerstone hunt, hasn't she?"

"Yes, sir," Joe said. "We started this morning. Have other students been by already?"

For a moment Mr. Potts didn't say anything. He was concentrating on pounding an iron peg into the fence post with a hammer. Then he wiped his face with a blue bandanna and said, "No, Joe, I haven't seen anyone else yet. You're the first so far. But about this time every year someone comes looking for the Willow Bend cornerstone, so it was an easy guess." He stood up and pointed down the road with his hammer. "Most of the search parties look about a mile in that direction, on either side of the bridge across the Willow River."

"We've got a different idea," Joe said. He introduced Sam and David. Then the kids explained that they were going to look at the place where the river had curved and then changed course. "There should be a crescent-shaped lake or pond on the other side," Joe finished.

Mr. Potts nodded. "Half Moon Lake. I know it well. It's down past my property, way off in the woods now. Don't know how you'd get there, though, unless you wanted to wade across the river."

"We think the town was on this side," David said. "Could we look there?"

"Oh, sure," Mr. Potts replied. "You can get there easily enough. All you have to do is go through the pasture, down the hill, and there you are." He scratched his head. "You know, come to think of it, I remember seeing some foundations down there near the river. Saw them, oh, a long, long time back."

"Where were they?" Sam asked, a new excitement in her voice.

Mr. Potts laughed. "I couldn't tell you to save my life, Samantha. That was thirty years ago, when I was just a little fellow. I used to go down to the river and catch frogs and crayfish. Sometimes my friends and I would play along the banks. Once we found what looked like some crumbling brick foundations in the weeds. My dad thought it might have been the ruins of an old mill. You know, gristmills used to be built beside rivers. Folks used waterwheels to turn the grindstones and grind wheat into flour."

David was looking at the cows. Six of them had wandered over and were munching grass near the fence. "Is it safe to go through your pasture?" he asked. "We're not going to get chased by a bull or anything, are we?"

With a grin, Mr. Potts shook his head. "These are all dairy cows. I don't keep a bull in this pasture. Besides, to tell you the truth, my cows all think they're pets. They may get nosy enough to come over and take a look at you, but they're gentle. In fact, I'll have to ask you to be careful not to startle *them*. Joe, your dog won't try to chase them, will he?"

Joe reached down to scratch Wishbone's ears. "He's a good dog, Mr. Potts. I think he'll be all right."

"Fine," Mr. Potts said. "Roll your bikes down to the gate and I'll let you in. But you kids be careful around the river. The water's not deep, but the ground's pretty flat along the riverbanks, and it's likely to be muddy."

"We'll be careful," Sam promised.

They rolled their bikes off into the pasture. At Mr. Potts's suggestion, they left them inside the gate. "You won't be able to ride your bikes down where the ground's soft," he said. "Besides, you'll have to climb over the fence down there. The fence is there to keep my cattle from getting stuck in the mud."

The group set off on foot. Wishbone was sniffing the ground. "Come on, guys! I smell water ahead. That must be the river." He swerved around a round, flat mass on the ground. "Whoa! Be careful, everyone. You've got to watch your step in a cow pasture."

They went over the top of a hill and headed down the far side. Ahead of them, a group of seven cows stood around a mossy stone drinking trough. One of them was drinking. She lifted her head, water running from her muzzle.

Wishbone heard the drip of water and realized he was thirsty, too. He trotted toward the cows. "Excuse me, but if you don't mind, I'd like a drink." Two of the animals stepped out of his way. "Thank you, ladies!"

A pipe brought a thin stream of water flowing into the trough. At the lowest point, the water overflowed. A stream ran down the gray-stone side of the trough, the only place not overgrown by moss. Wishbone lapped at it until he had satisfied his thirst. Then he set off after his friends. They were almost out of sight at the bottom of the hill.

Wishbone reached them just as they were climbing a wooden fence. He squeezed under it himself. His nose told him his friends had reached the river. He plowed under some weedy brush and got there a few steps before the others.

This part of the Willow River wasn't big. In fact, it was hardly more than a stream. It was no more than ten feet across and probably not even a foot deep in the middle. Wishbone sniffed. "Mud. Lots of mud. Hmm . . . The river isn't at its high point now, but this is all very low ground. I could see how it might seriously flood after a big rain. Lucky for us the sky is clear!"

Sam picked up a flat river stone and skipped it on the water. It hit twice, then went rolling off onto the far bank of the river. "Let's scout around," she suggested. She pointed to a thick stand of willow trees growing along the riverbank. "David, you check out the woods. Joe, you go east. I'll head west. If anyone sees any sign of those brick foundations Mr. Potts mentioned, yell out."

"Okay, but let's all be careful," Joe said. "Come on, Wishbone."

David picked up a fallen tree branch that was fairly straight. He used it to poke around the undergrowth as Joe and Wishbone set off. Joe had a hard time now and then, because the bank of the river was muddy and slippery. Sometimes he had to walk a few feet away from the bank, but he never lost his footing. Since Wishbone traveled on all fours, he didn't have that kind of problem, so he stayed close to the river.

Wishbone scouted ahead. The trees grew close to

the river there. In a shadowy, cool glade Wishbone smelled something damp and living ahead. He stalked it, deciding that whatever it was lay hidden in a clump of grass. As he edged toward it, something flashed through the air and landed in the river with a *plop!* Wishbone stopped, puzzled. He raised his ears high.

Behind him, Joe laughed. "You found a frog, buddy," he said. "But he's gone now."

Wishbone gave himself a good shake. "A frog. I knew that! I didn't think it was a leaping lizard. I wonder if there are any more of them around."

As Joe made his way through the underbrush, Wishbone sniffed his way along the bank. He caught the scent of another frog and crept forward, eyes alert. This time he saw it on the bank. A green frog with dark brown spots sat in a little puddle right at the edge of the river. Closer and closer Wishbone edged. He tried to see if he could sneak up on the frog. At first he thought he was going to get close enough to touch it.

But the frog was alert, too. First, it crouched down

low. Then it sprang through the air and landed with a splash in the river. Wishbone ran to the edge of the water in time to see the frog swim away. It kicked its long hind legs as it glided off. He barked once. Then, satisfied that he had protected Joe from the attack of the hidden tadpoles, he hunted for another frog.

He didn't find one, but he did see a pale crayfish swimming along the bottom of a still, little pool. It splashed a small amount of muddy water as it hurried past. Wishbone also spied a huge bird, a wading heron. It stabbed its beak into the water and came up with a silvery, dripping-wet fish. Then it flew away. Running along the bank, Wishbone enjoyed the feel of the cool, squishy mud beneath his feet. He liked the breeze in his face and the sound of gurgling water from the river.

Just about a perfect day, he thought with great satisfaction. *Even if we can't find the Willow Bend cornerstone.*

He took a step forward and then froze. He had heard something!

Wishbone whipped his head around, straining his ears. The sound was distant, but—

"Help!"

It was Sam's voice. She sounded as if she were in trouble!

Wishbone barked.

Joe stopped and looked back. "What's up, Wishbone? Find another frog?"

With a low bark, Wishbone looked around at him, then back the way they had come.

"Help!"

There it was again!

Wishbone barked again and started to run back.

Joe followed him. "What's the matter?"

By that time, Wishbone was running full tilt. "It's

Sam! She's yelling for help! There may be danger! Come on, Joe!"

Joe jogged along behind.

Once more Wishbone heard Sam yell, "Hey, guys! Help me!"

From the way Joe's running footsteps sped up, Wishbone knew his best friend had heard Sam, too. They ran to rescue Sam—but from what?

Danger! It was part of every adventure! As Joe and Wishbone rushed off to help Sam, Wishbone remembered how in *King Solomon's Mines* the adventure seemed to be all over. . . . Then danger raised its terrible head once more.

Chapter Eight

The battle began on the outskirts of the village, before the eclipse came to an end. We fought through the long afternoon. Infadoos quickly organized the warriors loyal to Ignosi into five regiments of two thousand men each. Each regiment ran to attack a stronghold of Twala's men. Our own group he called the Buffaloes. We attacked King Twala's personal troops, nearly three thousand fierce warriors. In fearless fighting we drove our enemy back.

Soon I was panting with effort. At one point, I thought we were soon to die. Eighteen of us, including Captain Good and myself, had been cut off. Fifty warriors charged us. With no time to reload our rifles, Good and I used them as clubs. The air was thick with the whistling of hurled spears. Desperate warriors slashed at us with *tollas,* their double-edged daggers.

Then I heard a shout to our left. I saw one of our other regiments, the Grays, running to our rescue. Caught by surprise, Twala's warriors fought for a few moments but then dropped like flies. The Grays charged past us and broke through the line of Twala's main army.

For a few minutes, there was nothing but confusion. I reloaded, fired, and reloaded again.

At last the fighting died down. Sir Henry, his yellow hair and beard gleaming in the light of the Sun, clapped me on the shoulder. "Where's Good?"

I raised myself high on the tips of my paws and looked around. "I don't know."

We searched for what seemed like an hour. Then, finally, Sir Henry laughed and pointed. Fifty yards, away, the short, heavyset Captain Good stood on a six-foot-tall anthill. His rifle was raised over his head in a sign of victory. Sunlight gleamed off his monocle. At the base of the hill lay many bodies of the enemy.

Then, to my horror, one of the "dead" warriors raised himself. He rushed up the hill. With his dagger, he stabbed at Good from behind. Good fell forward, and we saw the warrior stab him again and again, crying, "Take that, witch!"

We rushed forward, but the warrior fled. Sir Henry reached Good first. Ignosi pushed through the crowd and asked "Is he dead?" in English.

At that, Captain Good raised his head. Amazingly, his monocle was still in place. "Dead?" he murmured. "Not a chance of that! Fine armor, this is. Made a fool out of that fellow, didn't I?"

I quickly examined him. The chain-mail shirt had saved Good from a death wound, though he would be badly bruised. His most serious injury was a dagger gash in his leg. Some of Infadoos's men carefully laid him on a long shield that served as a stretcher. We carried him along like that.

The Sun sank in the west as we marched toward Loo. We passed whole bands of Twala's defeated men. They threw their weapons onto the ground and bowed in surrender. Infadoos led our regiment, with Sir Henry marching beside him. I was on Sir Henry's right. As we came closer to the kraal, I saw other lines of warriors approaching from many directions. They were all our men. They waved their spears high to show they claimed victory over their enemies. We had won. It was all over . . . or so I thought.

We reached the great space where we had seen the witch-hunt the day before. It was deserted. No, not quite deserted. I saw that on the far side, in front of his hut, Twala sat, with only one attendant: Gagool.

Despite all of his cruel acts, he looked so sad that I almost sympathized with him. Infadoos held up his hand, and the regiment halted. Then Infadoos pointed at Sir Henry, Ignosi, and me. The four of us slowly walked forward toward Twala.

He sat silent, his battle-axe and shield on the ground beside his throne. He sat so still that I felt the fur bristling on my neck. He had some trick waiting to spring on us. Something dangerous, no doubt. As we approached, he raised his plumed head slowly. His one eye flashed with fury, almost as bright as the great diamond tied to his forehead.

Gagool cursed us as we approached, but Twala waved at her to be silent. He gave Ignosi a bitter look. "Hail, O King," he said sarcastically. "You have eaten my bread. And now, with the white men's sorcery, you have defeated my army. What is my fate?"

Ignosi returned his stare. "The same fate you gave my father many years ago," he said sternly. "Twala, you sit upon my father's throne. Now I have come to claim it as the true king."

"It is well," Twala said. "I will show you how a king dies. But I demand the right every Kukuana king has in defeat. It is our law. You must let me die fighting—or, if I win, you must let me live."

Ignosi stood proudly. "Then take hold of your weapons. I will fight you."

Twala's face creased into an evil grin. "No, for it is also our law that the king cannot fight, except in war. I may choose someone to fight in your place." He ran his eye down our line. For a moment, I had the feeling he might choose me. I was not eager to face that powerful giant of a man in battle.

"Incubu," Twala said. The word meant "the lion." He pointed at Sir Henry. "Incubu, we shall fight to the death. Unless he is afraid."

Sir Henry had learned enough Zulu to understand that. His cheeks flamed red with anger. "We shall see who is afraid," he growled.

I put a paw on his arm. "Sir Henry! Don't risk your life against a desperate man! Anyone who saw you fight knows you are no coward."

Sir Henry said, "No living man will call me a coward. I will fight him. I am ready." He lifted his axe.

Ignosi said, "Fight not, my brother. You have been my good friend. If you should fall at Twala's hand, my heart would break."

"I will fight, Ignosi," Sir Henry said calmly.

After a moment, Ignosi nodded in a solemn way. "It will be a good fight," he said. He turned to Twala and shouted, "Behold, Twala, your death is ready for you!"

The ex-king laughed wildly and then stepped forward. For a moment the setting Sun clothed them both in fire. They were a well-matched pair. They circled each other, battle-axes raised.

Sir Henry made the first move. He leaped forward and swung his axe. Twala was just able to avoid the blow.

The heavy axe put Sir Henry off balance. Twala swung his own axe around his head and brought it down.

I wanted to put my paws over my eyes. I was sure Sir Henry was done for, but with a twist he raised his shield. The axe hit it and hacked straight through. It struck Sir Henry's shoulder, but it did no serious damage. In a moment Sir Henry had returned the blow, causing Twala to stagger.

Two warriors brought Captain Good to the edge of the fight on his shield-stretcher. He shouted out advice to Sir Henry: "Give it to him amidships, Curtis!"

Dust rose as the two men struggled. They grunted as they swung the axes, and they groaned when they fought off the blows. Then Twala struck not at Sir Henry, but at the iron-reinforced ivory handle of his battle-axe. The handle snapped short. With a roar of triumph, Twala threw down his shield and raised his weapon to kill his enemy! He swung and missed.

Sir Henry charged him. He threw down his shield. Then he wrapped his arms around Twala's arms and waist and lifted him off the ground. The surprised Twala could not use his axe against Sir Henry. He dropped it and pulled out his dagger. I saw him try to sink the dagger into Sir Henry's back—but the wonderful armor held off the blade. Howling with anger, Twala tried again and again to stab his enemy.

Sir Henry pushed away from Twala and pulled out his own dagger. He stood gasping, ready to continue the fight. Suddenly, Twala turned and grabbed a spear from Gagool, who had crept to that side of the circle. With a scream of anger, he raised his arm to skewer Sir Henry!

But Sir Henry had held onto his short battle-axe. He circled to one side as Twala charged. Sir Henry swung the axe around and it flew through the air! We heard a horrifying thud. Then Twala staggered and fell face down to the ground.

Gagool screamed in anger and terror.

Sir Henry lost his balance and fell himself. I ran to his side, afraid that he had received a mortal wound. His gray eyes turned to me, and he gave me a weak smile. "Just exhausted," he gasped.

I turned to Twala, who lay stone-dead. Taking the end of the leather cord in my teeth, I untied the great diamond from around his head. I took it to Ignosi and laid it at his feet. "There," I said. "Take it, lawful king of the Kukuanas."

Sir Henry slept for the rest of that day, and all through that night. I was beside him when he awoke. "Hello, Quatermain," he said. "My throat is awfully dry."

I fetched him a canteen, and he drank eagerly. "How are you?" I asked.

Sir Henry rose from his sleeping mat and stretched. "Very, very sore," he said with a groan. "How is Good?"

It was hard not to smile. "He is a hero," I said. "A charming Kukuana nurse named Foulata—yes, the same girl we saved from death—is taking very good care of him. He will limp for a few days, but I expect he will recover fully."

Sir Henry's face darkened. "I never killed a man like that before," he said. "Not face to face, not someone whom I knew."

"And you didn't this time, either," I told him. "You missed your stroke with the axe. It bounced off the king's chain-mail shirt. In another second, he would have tossed his spear right through your throat."

Sir Henry brushed his hair and began to dress. "I don't understand. He fell dead."

"He did, indeed," I told Sir Henry. "With Gagool's dagger in the back of his neck. She threw it at you. Twala leaped forward just as she threw it. So her evil act killed the wrong man."

"What's happened to her?" he asked.

"No one knows," I told him. "In the excitement, she got away. But without a king to do her dirty work, I'd say she's probably harmless now. Do you feel like eating some breakfast?"

"I could eat a hippo," Sir Henry said.

I gave him a dry smile. "In Africa, Sir Henry, be careful what you wish for," I told him.

The menu did not include hippo, but we had our fill of antelope steaks. Ignosi had been very busy. After breakfast, he sat on the throne in the same open place where the witch-hunt had been held. Once more, thousands of warriors stood there. They were Twala's men, and they obviously expected death.

But Ignosi stood and said, "Though you fought for my enemy, you fought well. I am now king of the Kukuanas. My ways are not Twala's ways. If you will promise me as proud warriors never to raise your spears against me, you shall live. Do you promise?"

For a long time, no one spoke a single word. Then a scarred old warrior lifted his head. "I knew your father, O King," he said hoarsely. "I welcome his son. I promise, my king!"

And that was like a dam bursting. In a moment, the others were shouting out their promises, too, and cheering the mercy of the new king. "We will make Kukuanaland a kingdom of justice once more," he promised. "No man—no, not even the king—can take your land or cattle without legal cause. And the days of witch-hunting are over. So says the king!"

The cheers were so loud I felt like putting my paws over my ears. But they were a good thing to hear. It was far different from the sounds of screams of terror that we had heard when Twala was king.

A week passed. With the help of his devoted nurse, Foulata, Captain Good recovered. He could walk with the aid of a stick. He soon became the center of attention. All the children of the Kukuanas flocked around him like so many chicks around a mother hen. He entertained them with magic tricks. Then, when he felt they should go home again, he would pull out his teeth. Then they all ran away screaming—but laughing at the same time.

Ignosi spent the week making decisions and solving the problems left over from Twala's reign. The people learned that they had a fair and just ruler again. I was pleased to see that our faithful friend Umbopa did not change once he had become King Ignosi. Though he now wore the leopard skin and headdress of the Kukuana instead of shirt and trousers, he remained our friend. He was still a gentleman, and I knew he would always remain one.

Finally, Ignosi asked us all to come to his hut. He had us sit on mats. Then he said, "Sir Henry—" He broke off and smiled. "Forgive me, brother. I cannot think of you as Sir Henry Curtis. I can only think of you as Incubu, the lion. Incubu, I know your heart aches to carry on with your quest, to find your lost brother."

Sir Henry bowed his head. "My brother Ignosi speaks the truth," he said simply.

Ignosi smiled. "You are always welcome here," he said. "And if cannot find your other brother, you have one forever in me." Then he sat up very straight. "My people have no memory of a white man such as Mr. Quatermain described. If your brother passed through our land, there is a small chance he might have made his way without being noticed. If he was heading for the mines of Solomon, then I can tell you exactly where you must look."

"And where is that?" asked Captain Good eagerly.

"It is called the Place of Death," Ignosi said.

I raised my paw and said, "Uh . . . excuse me? The place of *what?*"

"Then I must go there," Sir Henry said.

I waved my paw. "The place of *what?* Uh . . . I think I'll pass on this leg of the trip."

"We'll leave tomorrow," Captain Good said.

Ignosi nodded. "The Kukuanas cannot go there," he said. "It is a holy place for us. Except at certain solemn times, we must not enter it. But my hunters will tell Mr. Quatermain the way. It is at the base of the mountains called the Three Witches."

I stared at him. "The place is called *what?*" I asked again. "I'd rather not go, thanks."

"Then it's all settled," said Sir Henry, rising from his mat. "Thank you, Ignosi."

I sighed. No one was listening to the great white hunter.

Whether I wanted to go or not, it looked as if we were heading for the place of—well, you know what.

Chapter Nine

Ignosi's wise advisers gave me full directions to the Place of Death. Sir Henry was eager to be on his way, but I urged him to prepare well for the dangerous trip. "It will be a march of three or four days," I told him. "Let's wait until Captain Good can move around better, and until we've gathered food and water to see us through."

Sir Henry agreed. Even so, he was all fired up to start out. Ignosi's people supplied us with dried meats and gourds filled with fresh spring water. They also cautioned us about dangers on the way.

Captain Good took two days to recover, and then we set out on the morning of the third day. The captain limped along well enough, leaning on a staff for support. His devoted nurse, Foulata, wept to see us go, but we promised to return again.

Ignosi himself went with us a little way. "Let me warn you about one last thing," he said. "Gagool is still free. She hates you. Be on the watch for her."

"Should we shoot her if we spot her?" Captain Good asked grimly.

Ignosi shook his head. "Evil though she is, she has

great knowledge. I hold it a sin to kill knowledge. Avoid her, that is all. I will send my uncle Infadoos a day after you have left. He will follow your trail and make sure that Gagool is not also tracking you. We will perform the rituals of purification so that my uncle can wait for you among the huts that are at the base of the Three Witches. Beyond the huts you will find three great statues, and then the sacred Place of Death, which my uncle may not enter."

Ignosi said farewell to us when we reached Solomon's Great Road, and so did the other Kukuanas. Curtis, Good, and I walked ahead, following that ancient route. It stretched into the far distance. It seemed to dissolve slowly in shimmering waves of intense heat.

The surface of the road was firm. In some places trees grew, and the branches of the trees met above our heads. We walked through tunnels of warm green shade. Good pointed out that the Kukuanas had to clean the road. "Otherwise," he said, "it would be covered with centuries' worth of fallen leaves."

"Perhaps," said Sir Henry, "they think the road is sacred, like the Place of Death."

I felt my tail droop. "Sir Henry, you would do me a great favor if you simply called it 'our destination' from now on."

I had been right about the distance. Though Captain Good never once complained, he tired easily. We went only about fifteen miles the first day. We camped beside the road, near a clear little stream and under the shade of some tall trees.

Normally, I liked sleeping under the stars. The wide-open spaces were the finest bedroom any millionaire could wish for. The air was always fresh, and the ceiling sparkled with a million night lights. That evening, though, I felt jumpy. Some danger lurked nearby, but I could not sniff it out.

At my suggestion, we stood watches. Sir Henry took the first watch, and he woke me at midnight for mine. Our campfire had burned to red embers. I sat warming my muzzle at it, listening to the screeching of night insects. Once I heard the distant growl of a leopard, going about his business of hunting.

Then, seemingly almost directly at my elbow, a cackling voice burst forth: "Ha-ha! You go to your death, O Witch!"

I snatched up my rifle and stared into the ink-black darkness. "Gagool!"

The voice came from farther off, faint but clear: "Once a woman of my tribe showed a white man the way to the place where the bright playthings are. That man filled a bag with the sparkling stones, but he never took it away. Evil came to him. The woman who led him was named Gagool. Perhaps it was I."

The fur all along my back stood up straight. Sir Henry, who could sleep like a log, didn't even stir, and Captain Good only muttered in his sleep. "You're talking about Jorge del Silvestra," I told her. "He died three hundred years ago. You can't be that old!"

The evil cackling laugh came again. "Perhaps it was my mother's mother's mother who told me that story. Her name was Gagool, too! Or perhaps I *am* that old. We will see when you reach the Place of Death. They who wait for you there wait with hollow eyes, and the wind sighs through their empty ribs. Ha-ha-ha!"

The voice faded so slowly that I was half-convinced it had been a bad dream. But I was fully awake. More than ever before, I dreaded our journey and what lay at the end of it.

The next day we set out once again. After three or four miles, the road climbed a gentle rise. The landscape lay before us like a model. Straight as a ruler, Solomon's Great Road cut across a rolling plain to three distant mountains, sharp-peaked and almost frighteningly bare. Their streaked black sides rose steeply from the plain around them. "The Three Witches," I said, pointing.

Captain Good shaded his eyes. "Strange-looking mountains."

"Volcanic peaks," I told him and Sir Henry. "Ignosi's people told me that there is a small village of huts at the base of the first peak. That is where the Kukuanas stay on the rare times they visit the place. Beyond the village is the entrance to the mines."

"Two days now?" Sir Henry asked eagerly.

"About that," I said. We began to march.

That night we camped on open prairie. Even when I was not on watch, I kept my ears raised high for any sound of Gagool. I heard none. The next day took us closer and closer to our goal.

By evening, the mountains stood large and threatening above us. Their rugged slopes were lifeless, dead. Their peaks were snow-covered. Looking up, I saw streamers of white blowing from each summit. Five thousand feet above our heads, fierce winds were whipping the snow away from the rock. Despite the tropical heat, I shivered.

We came to the deserted village of six huts. That night we slept in one of those. Again, however, I had the jumpy feeling that Gagool was hiding somewhere nearby. I was still dog-tired the next morning when we set out on the last leg of our journey.

For an hour and a half we walked down the heather-bordered road. To our right the first mountain stood high, and ahead of us waited the other two. Looking ahead, I saw that the road seemed to come to an end, strangely, as if it had been cut off.

Soon I understood why. We walked until we stood at the very edge of a great round pit. It was like a crater dug out of the earth, at least a half-mile around. Its steep, sloping sides dropped down three hundred feet. Dozens and dozens of cavelike openings showed themselves in the crater wall.

"Well," I said, "I never believed that we would find them, but here they are."

"What?" Captain Good asked, sounding puzzled. "Great ugly holes in the ground?"

I said, "You've never seen the vast diamond mines at Kimberley. Sir Henry, Captain Good, you may be sure of this—we stand on the edge of King Solomon's diamond mines. See those worn, flat slabs there? That is where the ancients used to wash the clay they dug from the mines. They dissolved it until only the diamonds were left behind."

At the edge of the pit, the road divided and went to the left and right, around each side of the mine. Since we had not found George Curtis, we decided to circle the pit on the right. Soon we were almost all the way around the mine. In front of us, we saw three strange, tall forms.

"Statues?" Sir Henry asked, gazing up, his yellow beard fluttering in the breeze. "Idols?"

"They must be what Ignosi's wise men called the three Silent Ones," I told him. "Yes, idols, I suppose. The ones Twala sacrificed maidens to. The Kukuanas don't like to speak of them."

The figures proved to be statues of three seated people: two male, one female. The statues themselves were twenty feet high. But they stood on bases that raised them another twenty feet. With arms crossed, they gazed toward the road that led sixty miles to the distant pass at the twin peaks of Sheba.

"I don't like the two blokes," Captain Good said in almost a whisper, staring through his monocle at the statues. "The lady's all right."

The male figure on the right had the twisted, terrible features of a devil. The one on our left had a calm face, but it was the calmness of cruelty. The expression said: *I will watch you suffer. I will not enjoy it. But I will not help you, and I will not suffer myself.* The female figure had been worn smooth by the weather. Rising on either side of her head were the two points of a crescent.

"What do you suppose these statues represent?" Sir Henry asked.

"I'd say these were some kind of heathen gods," Captain Good said.

Then I remembered the Old Testament. "You are right," I said. "Solomon went astray, worshipping strange gods. Three of them were Chemosh, god of the Moabites; Milcom, god of the children of Ammon; and Ashtoreth, the goddess of the Zidonians. And, Captain Good, Ashtoreth, the lady, as you call her, isn't as nice as she seems. She, like the other gods, was worshipped in the old days by means of human sacrifice. These ancient gods are the three Silent Ones."

"Well, they cannot tell me anything about my brother," Sir Henry said. "That much is clear."

"Beyond these three Silent Ones is the Place of Death," I said, remembering what we had been told. "It is the last place we can look."

"Then let's go on," Sir Henry replied.

We passed the three statues. There the road was much narrower. It felt rough beneath my paws, as if centuries of rain, wind, and hail had chipped away at it. We had gone no more than fifty paces beyond the three Silent Ones. Then, suddenly, I saw that the road ended at a solid wall of rock. It rose almost straight up. Then it gradually slanted back until it became the slope of the central mountain of the Three Witches. Cut into the stone was an arched opening, like the mouth of a tunnel.

We walked toward the spot. Suddenly, like a ghost appearing from thin air, a human figure appeared in the archway, standing in the shadows.

We stopped. Then I heard the evil laughter of Gagool once more. "Why do you stop, strangers from the stars? You have reached the Place of Death! Have you reached your journey's end?"

Captain Good immediately raised his rifle, but Sir Henry placed a hand on his shoulder. Shouting to

Gagool, Sir Henry said, "We have no wish to harm you! But we are going to search this place."

Gagool came edging into the sunlight, her ancient eyes blinking. "Come forward," she said. "You will see the shining stones. Ha-ha! But let me help you. Let me show you the way. I alone know how to open the secret doorway. If I help you, you will tell the new king, and he will have mercy on me."

I translated what she said. Captain Good gave Sir Henry an anxious look. "Don't trust her, Curtis," he warned.

"Perhaps we should treat her kindly," Sir Henry said. "I'll bet no one else ever has. That may be the whole trouble with her."

"The whole trouble with her is that she's as sneaky as a snake," I told Sir Henry. "But it's your expedition. You must decide."

Sir Henry thought a moment. Then he said, "Tell her this: We will spare her life. If she helps us, we will tell the king. But if she tries to trick us in any way, we will strike her down with our magic."

I passed on the message, and Gagool laughed. "Then we have a bargain. If I seek your deaths, may I die myself. Come, witches from the stars. Come, you great warriors. I will do all your bidding and show you the bright stones."

"Lead on," I said. But just hearing her made my hide itch as though a family of fleas had settled in for a long vacation.

We followed her. Inside, the tunnel was just wide enough to let two of us walk side by side. Before long, we made our way in total darkness. Gagool's voice ahead of us acted as our only guide.

At one place I heard a whoosh of wings above my

head, and Captain Good cried out, "What just hit me in the face?"

"Bats," I said, thinking that being the right height was sometimes a bonus. "On we go."

The passage began to rise. Ahead I could see a faint gray light. It grew stronger. In a few moments, we stepped into the most wonderful place that the eyes of living men could ever see.

It was a natural cavern, as huge as a cathedral. The ceiling soared upward of two hundred, three hundred feet. It was windowless, but small natural openings here and there in the straight walls let shafts of sunlight in. Running in rows all along its length were gigantic white pillars. "Ice?" Sir Henry asked, touching one.

"Stalactites," Captain Good answered. "Solid feldspar! Look, the water is dripping from above. It must take thousands of years to form even one of these."

I didn't like the smell of the place. Gagool had gone on a hundred steps or so. She shouted and motioned to us. As we headed toward her, I could see that between some of the stalactites smaller caves opened off the main one. She led us to one of those openings. As we neared it, I could see it was man-made. The builders had chiseled a square door from the rock, perhaps enlarging a natural crevice. Gagool waited for us there.

When we approached, she asked, "Are you ready to enter the Place of Death?"

Captain Good must have guessed what she asked. "Lead on, Macduff," he said calmly.

"Perhaps you'd better go first, Quatermain," Sir Henry said.

I did not thank him for the thought, but I fell in behind Gagool. She went into the dark passage, a stick she carried tapping on the floor. Twenty paces on, the passage opened into a cavern forty feet long, thirty feet wide, and thirty feet high. Only one thin beam of light came in from an opening high in one wall. I could see that most of the room was taken up by a huge stone table. A shadowy giant stone statue sat at its head. Dozens of human-sized statues sat on either side, two-thirds of the way down the length of the table. Something dark was in the center of the table. . . .

And then I recognized it and yipped in alarm. Gagool lit a torch at that instant, and I heard Sir Henry and Captain Good cry out in surprise.

The thing on the table lay on its side. It was the corpse of Twala. It had been bent into a sitting position. Water dripped on the body from the ceiling. Already the skin was streaked with white feldspar crystals.

Twala's body was being turned into a stalactite!

Then I realized with horror that the human forms seated at the table were not statutes. These were past kings of the Kukuanas. All of them had been turned to stone! The gigantic statue at the head of the table was a grinning Death. For all eternity he ruled at that horrifying banquet!

"One last door," Gagool said. I shivered as we passed the stone table. She stood against what seemed like a solid wall of stone. "Behold," she said, pressing a spot on the wall.

Slowly a section of stone rose. It was like a portcullis, one of those large barred doors that could be raised or lowered to protect a castle's entrance. The stone made a rough grinding sound as it moved. Finally, it slid all the way up, revealing a doorway.

Gagool stepped through, carrying her torch. We followed. She stuck the torch into a carved-out hole in the rock inside the doorway. "Three hundred years ago," she said, "a white man came here. He gathered stones in a goat skin, but then something frightened him. He fled, taking with him only a small stone. It is the stone the kings of my people wear as a crown. That man died without returning. Until now, no one has returned. But now here you are." She laughed again and stepped aside to let us in.

A dark, shriveled goat-skin bag lay inside the doorway. Captain Good stooped and picked it up. It fell to pieces, but a shower of brilliant stones the size of marbles clattered out of it. "By Jove!" he exclaimed, picking up a double handful. "Diamonds!"

I looked around. We were in a vault dug out of the rock, ten feet square. More than a hundred ancient wooden boxes, stacks of them, lay against the far wall. Each box was eighteen inches long, a foot deep, and fourteen inches high. We went to them and found them all full of diamonds. None was smaller than a shirt button, and some were half the size of a hen's egg.

"Well," I said, "we are the richest three individuals in the world." I didn't feel rich, though.

"We'll flood the market with diamonds," Captain Good said.

"If we get to Europe with them—alive," Sir Henry replied.

"Hee! Hee! Hee!" laughed old Gagool behind us. "There are the bright stones that you love. Take as many as you would like. Go ahead and take them all! Eat and drink diamonds! Ha-ha!"

Good and Curtis were still ripping the rotten wooden lids off boxes, letting the sparkling diamonds pour out. I turned and saw Gagool pressing a spot on the wall. And I heard a grinding roar.

The stone door was closing!

Gagool ran for it. I ran after her, but I only succeeded in tripping her. Shrieking in fear and anger, she tried to roll beneath the lowering door and—

Crunch!

I couldn't even dare to look. I slowly picked up the fallen torch.

Captain Good and Sir Henry rushed to my side. "Crushed to death, by Jove!" the captain said. "Thirty tons of rock, at least."

"She promised that if she tried to bring death on us, it would fall on her, instead," Sir Henry said. "Well, it has happened."

"Worse than that has happened," I told him. "Do you know how to open the door?"

He looked at me, then at Good. We stared at one another in the flickering light of the torch, our expressions sick.

We had found King Solomon's diamonds, all right.

Only now we were entombed with them—perhaps until the end of time!

Allan Quatermain would agree that nothing was worse than facing disaster—unless it was not knowing what *kind* of disaster you were facing!

Similarly, Joe and I ran as fast as we could, both of us wondering what trouble Sam had landed in. . . .

Chapter Ten

As Wishbone ran full-tilt toward Sam's voice, David came crashing out from deep in the woods. "What's wrong?" he shouted.

"It's Sam!" Joe yelled back, a few steps behind Wishbone. "It sounds like she needs help! Come on!"

Wishbone didn't even look around. "This way, guys! Follow me! I'm hot on the scent! Uh . . . sound."

The river curved off to the right, and Wishbone followed its bend. By then he was ten yards ahead of Joe and moving ahead quickly. He burst through some tall weeds and skidded to a halt. Sam was in front of him, fifty feet away. She looked . . . short.

"Wishbone!" Sam yelled. She was waving her arms, as if trying to keep her balance. "I'm stuck!"

Wishbone took several careful steps forward. He felt the mud squish under his paws. Then he realized what was wrong, and why Sam looked so short. "You are knee-deep in mud. Hang on, Sam! I'll save you!"

Sam tried to pull her right foot free of the mud. That movement made her left leg sink even deeper.

Wishbone approached carefully, but when he was

still ten feet away, mud began to flow over his paws with a squishing sound. "Oops! Sam, how did you ever get that far out?"

Behind Wishbone, Joe and David came into sight. "Sam!" Joe yelled. "Are you all right?"

"I'm just stuck!" Sam yelled back. "Get me out of this glop."

David came as close to Wishbone as he could, then turned to Joe. "We can't get all the way out to Sam. If we try, we'll wind up stuck, too. Let me think of something."

Wishbone circled off to the left, but he could find no solid ground. "Looks like there's mud everywhere, guys! Even Sam's footprints are oozing back to mud."

"Stay still," Joe warned Sam. "If you move around, you'll just get stuck even worse."

"I already found that out," Sam told him. "I could see some bricks—they're right over there." She pointed, and Wishbone saw a low, crumbling line of old bricks ten feet in front of Sam. "I was trying to get to them and jumped over what looked like just a little puddle. Instead, it was a big mistake."

"Got it," David said. "What we'll have to do is get something to you, Sam. Then we can pull you out. A long, solid tree branch should do it. There are lots of them back in the woods. I'll go get one. Joe, you stay here and keep Sam company."

Joe had carefully come as close as he could to Sam. "I'm really sorry this happened," he told her.

Sam gave him a pained smile. "It's my own fault. I should have looked before I leaped."

Wishbone had made a wide circle. He finally reached the line of bricks and trotted along the top of it. He barked to get Joe's attention.

"Hey, look at Wishbone," Joe said. "He's closer to

you than I am, and he's on the bricks. Maybe we can get you out that way." He followed Wishbone's footprints, found some fairly firm footing, and made it to the bricks.

"Any sign of the cornerstone?" Sam asked.

Joe looked at the ruined foundation he stood on. "Nope. This may be part of Willow Bend, or maybe it's just the foundation of an old mill or a farm building that once stood close to the river."

Wishbone sat on the bricks and looked across at Sam. She had at least stopped struggling and sinking. He sniffed. "Too close to the river, if you ask me."

David came back, dragging a long tree branch. He had broken most of the small twigs off, so it was like a crooked pole about fifteen feet long. Joe showed him how to get to the brick foundation. Then, together, the two of them held out the branch so that Sam could get a good grip on it.

"Okay," Joe said. "Hang onto the branch and we'll pull you free."

"Here goes," Sam said. She held on tight, the boys

tugged, and her left leg came out of the mud with a squishy sound. She fought to keep her balance, then pulled her right leg free. One slow, squelching step at a time, she climbed out of the thick mud and got onto the brick wall.

Wishbone wagged his tail. "Way to go, Sam! You're free! You're rescued! You're . . . a mess."

"Yuck!" Sam said. "I'm a mess."

Wishbone blinked. "I just said that, didn't I?"

"You'll need to clean up," Joe told her.

Sam's jeans legs were soaked and caked with gray mud, and her sneakers were shapeless black lumps. She stamped off as much as she could. Then Joe, David, Sam, and Wishbone followed the line of the bricks away from the muddy spot. They came to the fence and plodded up the hill through the pasture. Water squirted from Sam's sneakers at every step.

Mr. Potts was at the top of the hill, running some water into the stone drinking trough they'd seen earlier. He saw them, waved, then looked closer. "Had an accident?" he asked, as they came closer to him.

"I took a bad step," Sam said.

"I should say you did," Mr. Potts agreed, shaking his head in sympathy. "You have to watch those low spots by the river. Well, I think we can clean you up a little, if you don't mind some cold water."

"Anything's better than this mud," Sam said.

"Slip out of your shoes," Mr. Potts told her. "They're sneakers, so water shouldn't hurt them. I'll hose them off. You can get up on the edge of the drinking trough, here, and rinse your jeans off. Don't worry about getting mud in the water. I'll drain it out and then fill the trough up again for the cattle."

"Okay," Sam said. Joe and David helped her climb

onto the edge of the stone trough. Then she swished her legs in the clean water. "This feels better already."

Wishbone dodged away as Mr. Potts squirted a stream of water on Sam's sneakers. He went to the other side of the mossy trough. "I'll stand guard here, Sam. Just in case any cows don't like you using their drinking water as a bathtub. . . . Hmm . . ." He noticed a place low on the trough where a patch of moss had fallen off. Carved into the stone were a couple of straight lines an inch or so long. Wishbone sniffed them. "What's this?"

"There, most of the mud is gone," Sam said. "Help me out, you guys."

Wishbone barked.

"Not now, buddy," Joe said, helping Sam climb off the side of the trough. "Easy, Sam. Don't fall."

"If only you'd listen to the dog. Okay, I'll do this my way." Wishbone began to scratch at the moss. It fell off the stone in green clumps. "More lines. I was right. Look here! Hey, look!"

Mr. Potts held up Sam's dripping sneakers. "Clean again. I think they'll be good as new once they dry."

Wishbone clawed a big patch of moss off the side of the trough—as big as his dinner bowl. "Look! You guys! Look at this!"

"Thanks a lot, Mr. Potts," Sam said. "Yuck! Well, at least now my jeans legs are just wet, instead of being caked with mud. You guys ready to go?"

Wishbone barked again and then rapidly started to claw at the moss.

Finally, Joe looked at him. "What's Wishbone doing?" he asked.

David craned his neck to see. "Looks like he's trying to dig into the stone," he said. "Easy, boy, Sam's all right. She's not in there anymore. Okay, let's head home."

Joe came around the trough and leaned over. He touched the patch of stone that Wishbone had cleared. "Hey, Wishbone's found something. Look at this."

Sam and David came to look, too. Wishbone had clawed away a good amount of the moss. The stained granite showed through. Some letters carved into the stone were visible:

Mr. Potts scratched his head. "I never noticed that before," he said. "'Course, that trough's been overgrown with moss for as long as I can remember. Here, let me get

119

a shovel or something." He hurried off and soon returned with a trowel. He used it to scrape away the rest of the moss, revealing more and more letters.

When he had finished, he stepped back.

"This is it," Sam said. "We found it!"

"*Wishbone* found it," Joe corrected, scratching his buddy's ears. "Good work, boy."

Now the inscription was clear:

A few minutes later, Joe hung up the phone in Mr. Potts's kitchen. "Miss Gilmore's coming right over," he said. "And, is she excited!"

Mr. Potts sat at the kitchen table and shook his head. "All these years, and I never suspected that. My dad never said a word to me about that drinking trough being special."

David said, "Maybe he didn't think it was, years ago. It was just a hollow stone that was good for cows to drink from, that's all."

Sam was drying her jeans legs with a thick towel. "I didn't know cornerstones were hollow," she said. "That threw me."

"Oh, sure," David said. "I've read about that. A lot of times when a building is going up, the workers use the cornerstone as a kind of time capsule. They put proclamations and current newspapers and things inside the cornerstone."

Wishbone sat on the floor, his tail thumping. "And I'll bet no one ever thinks that cows will use them as a drinking fountain."

Before long, Wishbone heard a car stop outside. Wanda Gilmore had driven up to the farmhouse in her beloved T-bird. She climbed out with her camera ready, looking excited. The kids came to the door with Mr. Potts when they heard her.

"Where is it?" Wanda asked.

Everyone trooped to the pasture, telling her the story as they walked.

Wanda looked at Sam in concern. "Are you all right?" she asked.

"Fine now," Sam told her. "Just a little damp."

"Here it is," Mr. Potts said.

Wanda stared wide-eyed at the drinking trough. "Oh, my goodness. You really found it. You really and truly found it!"

"Wishbone found it," Joe said.

Wanda raised her camera and focused the lens. "This is a red-letter day," she said. "This is—oh, Joe, your dog's in the way."

Wishbone was posing beside the cornerstone. "In the way? Wait a minute. Who scraped off the moss? Who nosed out the truth? Tell her, Joe! I'd tell her myself, but no one ever listens to the dog."

"Uh . . . Miss Gilmore?" Joe said. "Maybe you should take one picture with Wishbone in it. After all, he was the one who found the cornerstone."

Wanda laughed. "Yes, you're right. Okay, Wishbone. Say 'cheese'!"

Her flash unit went off, and Wishbone trotted over

to Joe's side as she took more photos. Many more photos, in fact.

When she had finished, Wanda said, "I can't wait to get these developed. Can I offer you a lift back to town, Samantha?"

"I've got my bike," Sam said. "I'm fine, really. We'll follow you back to Oakdale."

Wishbone led the way as the kids pedaled back toward town. They made the six-mile-plus trip in less than an hour. Of course, though, Wanda had made it back to Oakdale long before them. As the kids and Wishbone came down Oak Street, Mr. Gurney, who owned the local bookstore, waved at them. "Heard about your adventure!" he called. "Good going!"

Other people waved and gave their congratulations, too. Wishbone stepped high. "We're a success! There's nothing like an adventure that pays off. There's nothing like coming home a hero."

Even as Wishbone led Joe, Sam, and David through town, the triumphant terrier daydreamed again. He remembered how Allan Quatermain and his friends had to fight to succeed in their own adventure—one that had turned deadly. . . .

Chapter Eleven

"She's dead!" said Good, staring at the crushed figure under the rock door. "What a horrible way to go!"

"Don't waste too much time feeling sorry for Gagool," Sir Henry replied. "We'll soon be in a position to join her. Don't you see we have our own problems? *We're* buried alive!"

I knew that Sir Henry was right. That mass of rock had closed forever. The only person who knew its secret was crushed to powder beneath it. We could not force it open with anything short of blasting powder. And we were on the wrong side of it!

"This will never do," said Sir Henry. "Our torch will go out soon. Let's see if we can find the switch that works this thing."

I sniffed around the rocks. Nothing. I sat and thought for a moment. Then I said, "Don't even bother, Sir Henry. It won't work from inside. If there was an opening switch in here, old Gagool wouldn't have risked rolling under the door to escape. We're going to have to find another way out."

Sir Henry and Captain Good agreed. We made a

close search of the walls of our prison-house in the faint hope of finding some way to escape. We tapped both the walls and the floor, seeking some hollow place.

We didn't find anything. *Right,* I thought in disgust. *No one's going to have a back door to a treasure chamber.*

"I say," Good said in a strange voice. "Is it my imagination, or is the light from the torch growing dimmer?"

We all stared at it in sick fascination. The flame flashed and fluttered. Then it flared and showed the whole room in strong outline—the boxes full of diamonds, the goat-skin bag with its sparkling treasure spilled out, and the wild faces of the three of us, waiting to die of starvation.

Then the failing torch went out completely.

I don't want to think about how long we sat there in the darkness. I crouched in a corner, near the broken boxes, and played aimlessly with diamonds in the dark. We were buried alive in our living tomb, cut off from all the echoes of the world.

Ignosi and Infadoos would come looking for us—as if it would do any good. Even if they could find the door, I'd bet they didn't know how to open it.

A new Kukuana legend would be born. It would tell about how the old witch Gagool and the three white Sky Lords entered the Place of Death and vanished from the face of the Earth.

We had almost given up hope when an idea came up out of the darkness and hit me right on the muzzle.

"How is it," said I, "that the air in this closed-in place stays fresh?"

"Good heavens!" cried Good. "I never thought of

that! It can't come through the stone door. That thing's obviously airtight. It must come from someplace else. Let's have a look."

Amazing what a little hope could do. In a moment, all three of us were crawling around, feeling for a draft. We did that for at least an hour. Sir Henry and I were getting a bit discouraged. We kept knocking our heads against wooden boxes and the sides of the chamber.

We were lucky Captain Good wasn't ready to give up. It was he who finally found the faint breath of air coming up from a far corner of the room. It filtered through a layer of dust, but I could feel it lightly on my muzzle when I bent close. Sir Henry lit one of our few matches so that Good could see what he was doing. He stood and stamped down hard on a rectangular stone.

It rang hollow!

I've done some digging in my life, but nothing like I did then. The dust of centuries flew away until I'd uncovered a stone ring set in the floor. The captain scraped away at it with his knife. Then he carefully lifted the ring up from the floor. We all grasped the thing and—on the count of three—we pulled with all our might.

"Heave! Heave!" shouted Sir Henry. "It's giving. I can feel it giving. Heave! Heave!"

Then suddenly the stone came loose! We all fell backward, and the stone crashed to the floor, barely missing my paw. We scrambled up and found that where the stone had been, a dark, square opening led down into the earth. We had done it. I, for one, was impressed.

"Light a match, Quatermain," Sir Henry said, gasping. "Let's see what we've won."

I did and felt like a puppy. There, in the match's faint light, was the first step of a stone stairway. The treasure chamber had a back door, after all! "Of course," I said. "The mines! One way in to dig up the diamonds, and one way out for King Solomon's traders, who took them into the world. This must lead to the mines!"

"Now we have a chance," Sir Henry said. "Come on, lads, let's get under way. I'll go first."

"Watch where you put your feet," I told him. "We can't see the bottom at all. There may be some awful hole underneath us."

"More than likely just another room," muttered Good as he followed behind us.

It was just as dark on the stone stairs as it was in the treasure chamber, but at least we were moving. When we reached the bottom of the stairs, I lit another match. We were in a narrow tunnel carved out of the rock. Now, the question was, which way should we go? Right or left?

"The draft blows the flame to the left," said Sir Henry. "So we should go against it—air draws inward, not outward."

"Good thinking," I said, dropping the match before my whiskers caught fire.

So on we went, ever farther into the darkness. We wandered in a stone maze that led nowhere. Passages took sharp turn after sharp turn. We were in the mines themselves, the various shafts going different ways as the diamonds led the miners. We were getting exhausted and discouraged. Then a smell came up to me. I took a deep sniff and pricked up my ears. I could hear a loud noise, too. What was that sound?

"Sir Henry! Captain Good!" I howled. "It's running water! Do you hear me, men? It's water!"

"And that's our way out if we can just—" That was as far as Sir Henry got. I felt the earth beneath my paws dropping away. The whole floor fell away from underneath us, and we tumbled into a rushing underground river. Stones and dirt fell with us into the cold water. Fighting to make it to the surface, I dogpaddled for my life. Around me I could hear my friends swimming. Well, I could hear Sir Henry swimming. Captain Good was cursing so loudly that I had no idea what else he might be doing.

After what seemed like hours but was probably actually only a few minutes, we crawled up onto a low stone ledge.

"Well, at least we won't die of thirst," Sir Henry said, laughing. Captain Good muttered something awful, and I just panted. I shook myself and watched the water fly. I *watched* the water fly? Wait a minute. . . .

"*Light!*" I cried. It was so faint I almost doubted my normally sharp eyes. I jumped ahead. Yes! It was light! It streamed through a tiny hole in the packed ground. I started to dig like mad, dirt flying out behind me.

"Steady on, Quatermain!" Sir Henry cried. "Let us help you!"

The dirt under my paws was caving away. "No insult meant, Sir Henry, but I don't need your help. I think I'm about to break through— Oops!"

Then, for the second time that day, the earth gave way and we all went tumbling again. Only this time we were all falling forward. Then we rolled over and over through grass and bushes and soft, wet soil. I caught something, stopped, and called out. An answering shout came up from just below me, where Sir Henry's wild passage had been stopped by some level ground. I trotted down to him and we went looking for Good.

We found him jammed into a forked tree root. We freed him and then just sat there on the trampled grass, three bruised and muddy figures. But we were alive. The sky was streaked with gray light. We had been in the

Place of Death and the mines for more than twenty hours. Dawn was breaking.

Soon, the red sun rose. We saw that we were nearly at the bottom of the giant pit in front of the entrance to a cave. Above us towered the dim forms of the three huge statues that sat upon its rim. After a little more rest, we struggled up the sides of the pit, dragging ourselves along with the help of the tough roots and grasses growing on its sides.

At last we reached the top and stood before the three giant statues. In front of us burned a fire. I saw a sleeping form lying on the ground next to it. I recognized the gray hair and wrinkled face of Infadoos. As Ignosi had promised, he had sent his uncle after us, and our friend was waiting patiently for our return.

"We made it, lads," said Sir Henry, breathing a sigh of relief.

"And with precious little to show for it," said Good, polishing his monocle. "We'll never find our way back through that maze of tunnels and underground streams. Unless we can open that stone door—and I doubt we can—we've lost the mines forever, and all those lovely diamonds."

"Speak for yourself, my friend," I replied with a laugh. "Just before we left, I stuffed all my pockets with diamonds. Nice thing about my hunting jacket, shirt, and trousers—lots of pockets!"

It took us days to get our strength back. Then nothing could stop us from going back to the Place of Death to see if we could open the stone door. But we couldn't even find it. The wall was a seamless sheet of rock. It cut us off forever from the priceless treasures piled beyond. Gagool's door had become Gagool's tomb, and no one was going to disturb it. And, just as Captain Good had predicted, we could never hope to retrace our path of escape. King Solomon's mines were once more lost, this time perhaps forever.

Still, my old hunting jacket and trousers held enough glittering treasure to make us all wealthy. All in all, we hadn't done so badly.

We had an audience with King Ignosi and told him of the lost treasure chamber and the death of Gagool the Old. "And now, Ignosi, the time has come for us to say farewell," I said. "Tomorrow, at the break of day, will you give us an escort that will lead us across the mountains?"

"I have to think," said the king bitterly, "that it is the bright stones that you love more than me, your friend. You have the stones. Now you go to Natal and across the black water and sell them, as is the desire of the white man's heart. Well, you may go."

"Ignosi," I said softly, "tell us, when you were in Zululand, and among the white men of Natal, did not your heart turn to your native land?"

Ignosi nodded. "It was so, Macumazahn."

I spread my paws. "Then you understand. Our hearts turn to our land and to our own place."

Ignosi smiled sadly. "Your words are, now as ever, wise and full of reason, Macumazahn. The bird that flies in the air loves not to run along the ground. My brothers, you must go. My heart is sad, because you will be as dead to me, since from where you will be, no greetings can come to me. I will close the way to the shining stones to protect this land from the greed they awaken in men. But for you three the path is always open, for you are dearer to me than anything that breathes. My uncle, Infadoos, will guide you as you make your way. Farewell, my brothers and my friends."

He rose and looked sincerely at us for a few seconds. Then he threw the corner of his cloak over his head, covering his face from us.

We left in silence.

And so we set out from Kukuanaland with the loyal Infadoos. He told us there were two ways back out into the wide world. "You entered this land through the pass that leads to the Great Road," he said. "But the hunters speak of another way, to the north. That passage leads to a great oasis in the heart of the desert. It was once well known, but is now deserted. That will be an easier way to return. I will show you."

He led us to the pass. It was there that we said farewell to that true friend and strong, old warrior, Infadoos.

Good was so moved that he gave him his eyeglass. Actually, it was a spare one, but it thrilled Infadoos, anyway. He actually managed to secure it in his eye. It didn't look so good. I'm afraid eyeglasses didn't go well with leopard-skin cloaks and black ostrich plumes.

And then I came to perhaps the strangest thing that happened to us in our entire strange adventure. It was something that showed how wonderfully things could end. With Captain Good's leg fully healed, we made good time traveling across the desert. On the third day of our journey, we saw a green oasis far off. Then, on the fourth day, we reached it. As we entered the oasis, we saw under a fig tree a cozy little hut. I held up a paw, and behind me the other two men stopped.

"Infadoos said the oasis was deserted. Who could live here?" I said to my friends.

Even as I spoke, the door of the hut opened. Out limped a white man clothed in animal skins. He had an enormous black beard. It was impossible—no hunter ever came to a place like this, and certainly no hunter would ever settle there.

"Thank heavens!" the stranger said in perfectly good English.

Sir Henry looked and Good looked. Then all of a sudden the lame white man with the black beard gave a great cry and came hobbling toward us. When he got close, he fell down in a faint.

Sir Henry ran to his side. "Great Powers!" he cried, kneeling beside the fallen man. "This is my brother, George!"

George Curtis was unconscious for only a moment

or two. He opened his eyes and shouted, "Henry! Henry! It's really you!" Instantly, he rose. Then the brothers were slapping each other happily on the back. Whatever they had quarreled about in the past had clearly been forgotten.

"I thought you were dead!" Sir Henry shouted. "I have been all over the Suliman Mountains to find you. And now I come across you in the middle of a desert perched here like an old vulture!"

George replied, "I tried to cross the Suliman Mountains nearly two years ago. But when I got here a boulder crushed my leg. My guide, Jim, went for help, but I'm sure he died on the way. Otherwise, he would have returned. For almost two whole years I've been trapped here, unable to go forward or backward. I felt like a fool."

Then we were all laughing like hyenas, there in the middle of that unlikely oasis with that unlikely man. I wagged my tail until I thought it would fall off. We swapped stories, and Sir Henry showed his brother some of the diamonds. Then Sir Henry started to laugh again.

"By Jove!" George roared. "Well, at least you have something to show for all of your trouble, besides my worthless self!"

"They belong to Quatermain and Good," Sir Henry replied. "It was part of the bargain that they should share any reward there might be."

That set me to thinking. After a quick word to Good, I told Sir Henry that it was our unanimous wish that he should take a third of the diamonds. If he would not, his share should go to his brother. After all, he had suffered as much as we had for the chance to hunt them down. We finally got him to agree.

But we didn't tell George until we got back to Natal.

At this point, I shall end this history. Our journey across the desert back was long and hard. We had to help George Curtis along, for his right leg was very weak. The strain caused my old wound to act up, as well. But we did get through at last, safe and sound, though two of us were limping badly.

Six months later we all gathered at my little place near Durban. I am now writing there, curled up on my favorite rug, my own hospital stay over and my old lion bite healed again.

Here I will bid farewell to all who have accompanied me throughout the strangest trip I ever made in the course of a long and varied life.

And if you want diamonds, I'll be glad to tell you where they are.

But look for them yourself. It is the dream of all hunters in Africa to make their fortune—to save up enough to retire. I have more, much more, than enough. Tomorrow I'm bound for England to see my boy, Harry. And I'll also see about the printing of my journal, which is a task I wouldn't trust to anyone else.

Even the greatest hunts must finally end. And this, I think, is the end of mine.

Chapter Twelve

On Monday morning, Ellen Talbot walked to the foot of the staircase and called, "Joe? Can you come down here?"

Joe was getting ready for school. He stepped out of his room, still buttoning his shirt. "What's up, Mom?"

"I just wanted you to see Wishbone. Come and take a look at him."

The two of them walked into the kitchen. Joe laughed. Wishbone was sitting on the floor, his gaze on the refrigerator. "Maybe he's hungry," said Joe.

With a smile, Ellen said, "Well, Wishbone's *always* pretty hungry. But in this case, I think it's the picture."

The day before, Wanda had run an article about the discovery of the Willow Bend town hall cornerstone on the front page of *The Oakdale Chronicle.* Ellen had clipped out the story, which included a photograph, and had stuck it to the refrigerator door with a magnet. The photo showed Wishbone sitting as proud as could be beside the cornerstone.

"Yoo-hoo!"

The voice of Wanda Gilmore made Wishbone look

Canine explorer unearth...

around. Wanda was at the back door. Ellen quickly went to let her in. Ellen said, "We were just admiring your photograph, Wanda. Would you like some coffee? Some tea?"

"Oh," Wanda said, "a cup of tea would be heavenly, thank you." She stood behind Wishbone. "I don't know. Maybe I should have used one of the other pictures."

Wishbone blinked. "What? But this one is perfect! It's a great likeness of me. You can see the spots on my ear and everything. It's a very handsome photo."

"What's wrong with this one?" Joe asked.

Ellen poured a cup of tea for Wanda. Wanda said, "Thank you, Ellen. Oh, I don't think anything's exactly *wrong* with that photograph, Joe. It's just that some of the others showed the engraving a little more clearly, that's all. Wishbone's shadow is right across the 'T' of 'Town Hall' in this one."

Ellen laughed. "I think this picture is fine," she said. "You can still make out the inscription, and Wishbone looks very nice in the shot."

Wishbone felt his furred chest swell with quiet

136

pride. "Thank you, Ellen. I'm glad I'm not the only one who noticed what a great picture that is."

"Miss Gilmore, is the Oakdale Historical Society going to move the cornerstone?" Joe asked.

Wanda sipped her tea. "We haven't really decided that yet, Joe. Mr. Potts offered to donate it to the society, but I'd like to see if his father moved it or if it's in the original location. That's going to require some investigation. It's stood where it is for a long time. It won't hurt the cornerstone to stand there for a few more weeks or months, anyway."

The front doorbell rang. Joe went to answer it. In the meantime, Wishbone tilted his head, admiring the way his eyes looked so intelligent in the picture. "I look very distinguished in that photo. Very dashing. Almost like a—"

David Barnes came in and bent down to scratch Wishbone's ears. "Hi, hero!" he said.

Wishbone smiled at him. "Hero! Exactly what I was thinking, David."

"Where's Samantha?" Wanda asked. "She didn't catch cold from getting so wet, did she?"

David chuckled. "She's fine," he replied. "She's excited about school today. She, Joe, and I are going to tell the rest of the sixth grade all about how we tracked down the cornerstone."

Joe said, "Maybe we should take Wishbone to school, too. He was the one who scratched off the moss."

Wishbone sniffed. "Nothing any hero wouldn't have done, Joe."

"I wonder if he thought the cornerstone was something to eat," Wanda said. She added, "Or maybe he thought it was part of my garden. That's usually where he scratches and digs."

"The important thing is that he helped the kids find the cornerstone," Ellen said. "That's what makes him a hero."

Joe checked the clock. "Have you had breakfast yet, David?"

"Yes, thanks," David said. "But if you've got some juice, I'll have a glass while you eat."

"Sure," Joe said. He poured a couple of glasses of orange juice. He popped a few slices of bread in the toaster and poured himself a bowl of cereal. Then he turned and looked down at Wishbone, who was still studying the picture hanging on the refrigerator. "Well, hero," Joe said, "are you hungry?"

Wishbone glanced around and thumped his tail. "Joe, a hero is *always* hungry. . . . For fame! For glory! For adventure! For honor! For—"

Joe rattled a box of dog treats. "Here you go, buddy. How about a ginger snap?"

Wishbone jumped up, already licking his chops. "And especially for ginger snaps! I was going to get around to saying that."

When Joe tossed the snack to him, Wishbone caught it in midair, in true hero style.

About H. Rider Haggard

Sir Henry Rider Haggard, born in 1856, was the sixth son of an English landowner. He was educated in England, but as a young man he traveled to South Africa. He lived there for six years, serving as the secretary to the governor of Natal, a province of South Africa.

In Africa, Haggard got to know the ways of both the Africans and the Europeans who settled there. He came to respect the Zulus, a proud group of fearless warriors who later fought a hotly contested war against the British. Haggard came to realize that Africa was a wonderful setting for stories of high adventure. It was a land where danger lay with the animals, the beautiful and varied landscapes, and sometimes the people.

When @aggard became a writer, he devoted several of his books to factual accounts—histories, essays, and commentaries about Africa and other subjects. Finally, though, he turned to writing stories of adventure, and it was with that kind of book that he found his true calling. Over his long career, Haggard wrote nearly sixty books in all, and thirty-four of them were novels of adventure. He was an expert at creating the twists, turns, and cliff-hanging endings of the adventure story.

He also had a way of showing how fascinated he was by Africa. Haggard worked hard to describe the continent's peoples, landscapes, wildlife, and vegetation. Mixing large doses of his vivid imagination with his expert knowledge of Africa, Haggard brought his characters to life and sent them off on truly hair-raising escapades.

Other writers, including Rudyard Kipling, were his

friends, and they praised his literary abilities. Haggard received knighthood status in 1912, but he felt his true reward was knowing that he pleased and entertained millions of readers over the years. He died in 1925.

About *King Solomon's Mines*

Lost treasure! Unknown Africa! Adventure! All these elements have stirred the imaginations of readers for generations. H. Rider Haggard first began to write *King Solomon's Mines* on a bet. He was wagering that he could write an adventure story that would be as popular as Robert Louis Stevenson's classic tale, *Treasure Island*. He succeeded and won his bet, all right.

Beginning with a legend that goes all the way back to the Old Testament, Haggard spun a yarn about fabulous mines hidden far away from civilization, in the land once ruled by the queen of Sheba. According to the old tale, the wise King Solomon brought riches all the way from there to the Holy Land. But eventually the mines were lost, and for thousands of years no one could find them. . . .

No one, that is, except a bold adventurer like Allan Quatermain. Haggard's fictitious hunter is an unlikely hero. He admits that sometimes he is afraid. He even calls himself "a bit of a coward." Underneath that facade, though, Quatermain has true courage. He possesses the ability to face his fears and still do what must be done. The combination of his abilities and his modesty serve to make him a most likeable character.

Readers were so enamored of Quatermain, in fact, that Haggard brought him back for more adventures in later works he wrote. And H. Rider Haggard continued to pen classic tales of adventures: *She*, *The People of the Mist*, and many others, the majority of them set in Africa.

About Brad Strickland

Brad Strickland has written or co-written nearly forty novels, many of them for young readers. He wrote two books for The Adventures of Wishbone series, *Salty Dog* and *Be a Wolf!*; with his wife, Barbara, he wrote *Gullifur's Travels* for the same series. With Thomas E. Fuller, Brad co-wrote five titles in the WISHBONE Mysteries series: *The Treasure of Skeleton Reef, Riddle of the Wayward Books, Drive-In of Doom, The Disappearing Dinosaurs,* and *Disoriented Express.* Brad and Tom also co-wrote *Jack and the Beanstalk,* for the Wishbone: The Early Years series. Additionally, Brad writes the popular mysteries in the series begun by the late John Bellairs. His latest mystery hardcover is *The Wrath of the Grinning Ghost.*

When Brad isn't writing, he teaches English at Gainesville College, in Gainesville, Georgia. He and Barbara have two children: a daughter, Amy; a son, Jonathan; and a daughter-in-law, Rebecca. Brad likes traveling, sailing, photography, and acting in his college's theatrical productions. He was recently in Charles Dickens's *A Christmas Carol.* He has also acted in radio plays (once, by the way, he played a dog).

Brad and Barbara have many pets, including ferrets, cats, and two large dogs. The dogs are both diggers, and they've tried hard to turn the Strickland backyard into their own version of King Solomon's mines.

About Thomas E. Fuller

Thomas E. Fuller has co-written five WISHBONE Mysteries and one Wishbone: The Early Years book with his friend Brad Strickland. However, this current title represents the first time he has worked on a book in The Adventures of Wishbone series. Writing a story inspired by H. Rider Haggard's *King Solomon's Mines* was Thomas's idea. He's always enjoyed stories of high adventure in dangerous and strange lands—the kind of book the British like to call a "ripping yarn."

In addition to writing novels and stories, Thomas is the head writer for the Atlanta Radio Theatre Company. He has written close to twenty original plays, and more than forty audio dramas. His radio dramas have won the Mark Time Award twice, and they include adaptations of classic stories like H. P. Lovecraft's "The Dunwich Horror"; and original adventures, including one radio series, "The Lost Gold of the Atlantimengani," which, in spirit, is very close to the African-themed novels of H. Rider Haggard. Thomas's wife, Berta, is an artist and also a writer, with two novels to her credit.

Thomas teaches creative writing, and he also works for Barnes & Noble. He and Berta live with their children—Edward, Anthony, John, and Christina—in a cluttered blue house in Duluth, Georgia. They share their home with stacks of audiotapes, books, scripts, and paintings. All this is overseen by a puppy, Pugsley, and a large yellow cat, The General—who thinks *he's* really the one in charge.